FOOTPRINTS
OF
A GUNFIGHTER

COLE TURLEY

Copyright © 2023 by Steve Sisney

All rights reserved. No part of this publication may be reproduced, stored in a retrieval system or transmitted, in any form, or by any means, electronic, mechanical, recorded, photocopied, or otherwise, without the prior written permission of both the copyright owner and the publisher, except by a reviewer who may quote brief passages in a review.

The scanning, uploading, and distribution of this book via the Internet or via any other means without the permission of the publisher is illegal and punishable by law. Please purchase only authorized electronic editions and do not participate in or encourage piracy of copywritten material.

This is a work of fiction. Names, characters, places and incidents either are a product of the author's imagination or are used fictitiously, and any resemblance to actual persons, living or dead, business establishments, events, or locales is purely coincidental.

This book may contain views, premises, depictions, and statements by the author that are not necessarily shared or endorsed by Outlaws Publishing LLC

For information contact: info@outlawspublishing.com
Cover design by Outlaws Publishing LLC
Published by Outlaws Publishing LLC
July 2024
10987654321

On a hot July day in 1863, twelve Union soldiers lay trapped in a small ravine in the middle of a battlefield outside of Gettysburg.

They were unable to move because of sniper and cannon fire so they huddled together without water and little ammunition. Five of the men were wounded with one needing immediate attention. They had been separated from the rest of their platoon.

Sergeant Turley watched from a safe distance, with the rest of the platoon, trying to figure out how to get his men out of the death trap. He discussed with the Company Captain a plan to move east along the ridgeline of the mountain, out of rifle range, making it appear as if they were trying to outflank the Confederate forces.

Earlier that morning, Turley had instructed his men to build a wagon that had high sidewalls so the driver would have a place to take cover. He took that wagon and six horses and waited until the Confederate forces turned their cannons towards the company of Union forces. He then rushed toward the small ravine to rescue his men. By the time the Confederate forces realized that the movement along the ridgeline was just a decoy, he had the soldiers rescued from the ravine, loaded in the wagon and was headed back across the battlefield.

As Turley and his men raced across the battlefield towards the Union line, a cannonball landed in front of the wagon, killing the two lead horses. One of the men jumped out of the wagon and cut the harnesses from the two dead horses, freeing the four remaining horses which allowed the wagon and the men to reach the Union line.

Chapter 1

Sergeant Cole Dyami Turley had been in many battles, but nothing quite like the battle at Gettysburg, the bloodiest and largest battle of the Civil War. He had gained the respect of his men who he had fought with. Now, almost two years later, the war was finally over. The sun was just coming up to start a new day, when he dragged his big framed body off the army cot.

Turley was a large man with broad shoulders, who stood six feet and four inches. His skin was a cream coffee color and, with his brown eyes, most women considered him a handsome man. He could not remember the last time he had slept so well. Today was the day Cole Turley was getting out of the Union Army. The Civil War had divided his family with his brother, Luke, and brother in-law fighting for the South. Cole washed the sleep out of his eyes and went to get some army chow before he headed to the supply sergeant to turn in his army gear. The big, heavyset supply sergeant was already sweating from the morning heat.

He took his gear and told Cole that the colonel wanted to see him before he left for Indian Territory to see his sister. The colonel was not a tall man. He had grey hair and steel blue eyes, who had taken a liking to the Sergeant. He had arranged a farewell party for Cole because he couldn't talk him into staying in the Army. Cole and the colonel had been in a lot of battles together, the biggest one was at Gettysburg, where some of the bitterest fighting happened on three hot summer days of July 1° through July 3r, 1863, when Cole was accidentally reported as killed in action while trying to save a squad of men. Somehow it was reported Sergeant Turley was killed when it actually was Sergeant Thomas, one of the men at the ravine, who was killed. One of the men that Sergeant Cole Turley had saved that day at Gettysburg, was present along with his father.

The father was so grateful to Cole for saving his son, he presented him with two ivory-handled 1851 Navy Colt revolvers with his name engraved on them. He also gave him a 577 caliber repeating rifle. And, finally, he gave him what Cole liked the most - a big black Morgan horse with white on his forehead. The big horse stood close to sixteen hands with a graceful neck and a strongly muscled body. The Morgan horse had a reputation as a great cavalry mount during the Civil War. At first, Cole refused the gifts, but the soldier's wealthy father was so hell bent on him having them that he accepted them with gratitude.

After thanking the colonel and the grateful father again, Cole saddled his horse and headed for Indian Territory to find his family. Cole's grandfather was Irish and he had married a Cherokee Indian woman after his first wife had died. The Cherokee woman helped raise eight-year-old Cole and his brother and sister after Cole's parents were killed in a mysterious fire when Cole and his siblings were away from home. His grandfather had given Cole his first name which meant warrior' in Ireland; but his mother being part Ute Indian and black was not to be outdone - so she added Dyami to his name which means 'eagle' in Native American. Cole wanted to make peace with Luke and visit his grandparents.

As he rode the big black stallion, Cole suddenly realized he needed a name for his horse. It had to be a name that would fit the American breed that was known for its endurance, heart, and courage.

Traveling alone was dangerous with the war just over so Cole was extra careful to trust no one. Just outside of Kansas, on a lonely trail, he met two men who looked like they were up to no account. Cole just tipped his hat with the other hand close to his Navy Colt revolver and rode on past them. He had a funny feeling he would see them again. He found a good place to camp by a creek and big rocks in case they were going to try to ambush him that night. Cole built a campfire to make him some coffee and then laid out his bedroll.

After watering his horse, he unsaddled him and staked him out in a field of green grass close by. He let the fire die down, then went over to his bedroll and stuck some old clothes and other items into it. Cole took his hat off and placed it at the head of the bed role. Cole lost himself in the shadow of rocks with his back against the big rock and waited. Before daybreak his horse started snorting and pounding his leg letting Cole know something was out there. Cole watched the two men creep closer to his campfire. Both men stood up and started shooting into his bedroll as they walked into the camp. There was no time but to shoot to kill them both or they were going to kill him. Gun smoke filled the air while Cole walked over to where their bodies lay to check to make sure they were dead. He was right - it was the two men he had passed on the trail. Cole laid down by the fire to get some sleep. It was not the first time that he had slept with dead people and probably not the last time.

Before he fell asleep, he looked over at his horse and told himself that he had one hell of a horse.

The following morning, he thought he should leave their bodies for the buzzards since that was what they had planned for him. Not having a shovel to bury them, Cole decided to take them to the next town about twenty or so miles down the trail. First, he searched their pockets for money to bury them or some kind of identification. Between both of them, he only found about ten dollars. Cole started having second thoughts about reporting it to the sheriff, in case they had family in town, because he was not looking for any more trouble. But it was the right thing to do, so he tied them to their horses and rode toward town.

Chapter 2

When Cole got to town, the sheriff was sitting in a chair in front of the jail. He was a man in his fifties with a pot belly, mustache and sideburns. When he got out of his chair to examine the bodies of the two men, Cole noticed he limped on his right leg. Cole told the sheriff they'd tried to ambush him back on the trail. The sheriff glanced at Cole telling him he believed him because one of the men was wanted for murder and robbery with a 500-dollar reward on him.

The sheriff said, "Mister, he's got three brothers who will want to kill you for killing their brother.?

The sheriff then yelled for his deputy, who came running out of the jail, to take the bodies to the undertaker down the street. By this time a small crowd had gathered so the sheriff asked Cole to step inside to make out a report for his records. Sitting in his chair, he looked up at Cole and told him that to get the reward he would need his full name and would have to sign a statement. Cole told him that he had no problem with that. He was not looking for trouble but he figured it didn't matter if he took the reward or not; he still had to deal with the three brothers.

"Listen," the sheriff said. "I'm not a friend of the family, but I don't want my town shot up. It will take three days of hard riding to get to their ranch and three days back to town.

I will try to get your money in three days, but you got to promise me as soon you get the money you'll ride on. It's not one family, but an army you will have to deal with."

The sheriff paused and then said, "If it means anything, you did this town a favor. But I can't lose any more families to those cold-blooded killers. Our town orphanage is full of children whose folks tried to stand up to them. I can tell you, without a doubt, they control this town. Wearing those union pants won't help either."

Cole started for the door, saying "Well it beats nothing at all."

He led his horse down the street. At the stable he told the redheaded boy with freckles to give his horse a double order of oats and a good rub down. Cole asked the boy where a hotel was at. The boy just pointed the way.

Cole said, "If my horse tells me you didn't take proper care of him, I'll be talking with you to find out why you didn't."

After Cole checked in, he took a hot bath. He had to put his dirty clothes back on because the two men had shot holes in all his extra pairs. Cole asked the clerk if there was someone who could wash clothes for him.

The clerk told him to leave them outside his door and his wife would wash them for a fee.

Cole said he would in about an hour, but first he was going to get himself a drink of whiskey.

Walking into the saloon, he noticed the talk had been reduced to whispers and all eyes were on him. He ordered some whiskey from the bar, feeling the tension in the room. As he took a big sip of whiskey, he saw, out the corner of his eye, people starting to move away from the bar until only one man stood facing him. Cole studied him for few seconds and turned up the rest of his drink. The man wore his guns low, like a gunslinger and stood close to six foot tall. Acting like he didn't notice him, Cole turned his back to him hoping the gunslinger would not shoot him in back with all the people in saloon. Cole needed to locate tie second man in the room, hoping there was only the two. Yelling at the bartender for another drink to make them think he was getting drunk. He saw the second man, who was heavy set, with black greasy hair.

The slim gunfighter yelled out, "There's a rotten smell in the room. It must be a lowdown, yellowbelly Yankee in the room."

Cole just sipped on his whiskey as if he did not hear him which made the gunslinger mad.

"Hey, I'm talking to you!" he shouted. He then slid his glass down the bar where Cole was drinking. Grinning, the gunslinger said, "After I kill you, those fancy guns are mine. Nobody has ever beat me in gunfight. I'm Nate Collins, have you heard of me, Mister?"

Cole faced him where he could see the second man.

"Has anyone ever said you talk too much, Nate, especially with someone backing your play?"

The gunslinger's face turned red with rage, Mister, I am going to let you draw first. I'm going count to three and if you don't draw before I get to three, I'm going to kill you!"

Cole grinned and said, "Well, Nate, I'm impressed that you can even count to three." Nate's gun had not even cleared his holster when a bullet struck him in the heart.

Cole swung around, returning the gunfire from the second shooter, striking him in the head.

Gun smoke was still in the air when the sheriff rushed in to see what had happened. A crowd gathered around Nate's body and someone said, "I didn't think anybody could beat Nate Collins to the draw."

The sheriff came over to Cole and said, "I'm sorry but I didn't know Nate was in town or I would have warned you. Nate was a friend of the three brothers. Come on over to the jail. I need to fill out some more paperwork."

Walking over to the jail, the sheriff told Cole that he should be ready to leave town in the morning, some of the leading citizens would pay him the reward money out of their own pockets so he could leave. The townspeople would wait until the actual reward was paid to get reimbursed. They wanted Cole out of their town quickly so the town wouldn't get all shot up. The sheriff would tell the brothers that after Cole killed Nate, he decided his life was worth more than the reward so he left town. Cole said that was fine with him because he was not looking for any more trouble but he wanted the fine citizens to meet him at the Jail. Cole stated he also wanted the person who ran the orphanage outside of town to be there, too. It they wanted him to leave in the morning, they had better all show up.

The sheriff stared at Cole as he reached for the door. Walking out, Cole told the sheriff he would be in his room when he got all of them together.

Cole put a chair under the door knob and stretched out on the bed to take a nap. About three hours later, with the sun already down, someone knocked on the door. It was followed by the sheriff's voice so Cole moved the chair to the side. Opening the door, the sheriff told him everyone was at the jailhouse. Cole followed the sheriff to the jail house. He noticed there were six men sitting around his desk. When they saw the sheriff, they demanded to know why they all had to be here.

Cole did not answer, he only gave orders, asking which one had the general store. One short bald man in his sixties raised his hand.

Cole gave him a list of things he needed.

"Okay, which one has the reward money?" barked Cole.

A heavyset man in a suit, looking very much like a banker, handed the money to Cole, who started counting the money.

As Cole started counting the money, the banker barked, "It's all there!"

Cole gave the banker an icy stare before he said, "You should always double check. Now which one runs the orphanage?"

A slim man in his forties with thinning hair said, "I do."

"Well," Cole said, "I would like to make a donation," handing him four hundred dollars.

I would give it all to you but I need to pay for my supplies. Now we need to get our stories right before someone gets killed. When they get here, tell them my name and which way I went so nobody will get hurt. Tell them I left without the money - that way you will all be safe. I will be heading out as soon as I get my supplies on my horse. Any questions?"

The heavyset banker said, "We all thought you wanted the money for yourself."

Cole said, "I figure all of them will come after me if they think no one in town helped me."

Chapter 3

Cole was glad to be on the trail again with his horse. He had missed talking and whistling to the big horse. He and his horse were forming a special bond with each other. It was a full moon and the stars were hanging low in the still night, as they headed for the Indian Nation. It would be nice to see his family again after six years. His grandfather was a man always on the move looking for that pot of gold. The longest he had ever stayed anywhere was the Indian Nation, but he figured Mary, his second wife, had something to do with that since she was a full blooded Cherokee whose family lived close by. Her real name was Elakshi, meaning woman with bright eyes, but Grandfather had a hard time pronouncing her name so he called her Mary. She was just like a mother to Cole, his sister, and his brother. She had raised them as her own after Cole's parents had been killed.

Cole had a lot fond memories of growing up with her family in the Indian Nation. He also spent time with his mother's family, the Ute Indians of Colorado. The name Ute means land of the sun.' His grandmother married a black man who was a fur trader. He was killed when his mother was four years old in a gun fight over furs. With his mother being half black and half Ute Indian and his father being Irish, the family moved around a lot until they were killed in a fire. Now Cole was bringing more trouble to them; he had to get rid of three brothers and their army before he headed for his sister Sarah's home over close to Tahlequah. The Cherokee Indians had built a Cherokee Supreme Court Building in the town in 1844. The name Ahlequah was a Cherokee name meaning two is enough.' Cole didn't want to burden his sister with his problems, so he headed his horse towards Dodge City. He would hole up there to see how many were following him while he did some drinking and gambling.

When evening darkness came, Cole made camp by a little pond at the base of the hill. He built a campfire, with what little wood he could find, and made some coffee to go with his beef jerky for a supper meal. He turned his horse loose to eat the green grass around the pond. Cole had been working with his horse, so when he whistled, the big stallion came. Cole never had a horse like this Morgan; the horse learned quickly. Stretching out on the bedroll, with his guns close by, he stared into the night. Soon he drifted off to sleep.

Around midnight, his horse was snorting and he pushed Cole off the bedroll with his big head.

Jumping up, Cole noticed a pack of wolves coming down the hill. They had come for water, but when they saw the horse, it looked like an easy meal for them. Cole fired his rifle, killing the leader of the pack and two others before the wolves rushed back up the hill. Gunfire didn't even make the big black stallion twitch.

Cole patted him on the forehead. Yes, he had a very special horse. Cole stayed up for a while in case the wolves decided to come back. Watching and listening in the darkness seemed so peaceful now. Cole wished he could head for his sister Sarah's home to see her and his family, but he was not sure he was welcome because her husband along with his brother, Luke, had joined the Confederacy while Cole had gone north to fight for the Union. He remembered the stories his mother told about her family being slaves. Cole figured nobody deserved to be a slave. His grandfather understood a man needed to fight for what he believed in.

Cole's mind wandered back to a happier time when he was fourteen and his first love. She was a niece to Mary, his grandfather's wife. Ruth was a beautiful, Cherokee Indian girl. They had only kissed each other until that day everyone went to town, leaving Cole behind to watch the place and care for the animals. They had left early to get back before dark. Ruth had come by to go to town with them, but had gotten there too late. Seeing that Cole was the only one home, she started to leave when he grabbed and kissed her. Ruth ran to the barn, climbed up in the hay loft with Cole following her. What started out playing around ended up being a hot lust for each other's body. It was the first time for both of them. Afterwards, it started raining on the tin roof as they lay beside each other listening to the rain. It was a long time before Ruth spoke with tears running down her cheeks. Her family demanded that she marry someone of her own blood. It was very important to her family. When Ruth left that afternoon, Cole did not see her again because the family sent her to live with her grandmother and no family member would say where that was.

Sensing Cole was daydreaming, the big stallion nudged him with his head. Cole laughed and patted him.

"Okay, big boy, we'll go."

Chapter 4

The wind blew strong the next day as they pushed hard to reach Dodge City only stopping for a short rest. Cole and his horse should be in Dodge later that night and hopefully beat the storm that was moving in.

It was past ten o'clock when Cole reached the stables in Dodge City. A short bald man took the stallion and led him into a stall. "Mister, you and your horse look plum tuckered out. My name is Ed and for a dollar, I will give your horse a good rub down."

Cole flipped him a silver dollar, and told him to give him a double order of oats, also. He patted the big horse for he had earned it. Gathering up his gear, he headed for the hotel. Cole slept in the next day while the rain beat against the window pane. It was one of those days if you had a good looking woman, you would have stayed in bed all day, but Cole did not. He walked over to the barber shop for a shave and bath after he stopped in the general store for a shirt and pants.

After he got some chow, he stopped to check on his horse. The owner of the stable was looking at his big black horse when he walked in. He told Cole, "I have never seen better horse flesh than that big black." The owner was a tall, slim older man with gray hair and he walked with a cane. "If you ever want to sell him, let me know because I will give you top dollar for him."

Cole smiled and to the old man said, "How can you sell something that is a part of you? We were destined to be together."

The old man said, "I understand," asking Cole where he got such a fine animal.

Cole showed the old man the papers where he got the big black Morgan and his pedigree. The old man's face turned ash white, glancing around to find a place to sit. "All my life, I have been looking for such a horse. I will pay you five hundred dollars for stud service and I will take care of him." Cole told the old man he did not know how long he would be in town, but if he promised to have the horse ready to go on a moment's notice and give him 250 dollars for now, it was a deal.

The old man stood up to shake hands with a promise that Cole could count on him. The old man said, "My friends call me Ben. Oh, what is the stallion's name?"

Cole patted the head of the big black steed. "Well, I have been trying to come up with a good name since I got him. Now I am going to play some cards. How about Blackjack? Do you like the name, big boy?"

The stallion's head went up and down to agree. Turning toward Ben with a grin, he said, "His name is Blackjack. Hey Ben, which saloon is the best one?"

"That would be the 'Merry Gay' down the street," Ben told him.

Cole liked playing cards as long as someone was not cheating. He knew enough to spot a crooked game. Entering the saloon, he walked over to the bar and ordered a drink while he studied the room. He saw one cowboy acting drunk, hanging close to the card table. He was a spotter, giving signals to the silk shirted man who was the big winner. Cole kept a bowie knife in his right pant leg, reaching down, he unlatched it in case he might need it...

He ordered another drink, watching the poker table. The girl in the red dress was also giving signals to the heavyset man in the silk shirt.

With six men playing cards, Cole watched to see if one of players might be in on the cheating. One man on the right side of the man with the silk shirt, kept messing with the cards. No one paid him much attention since he was losing, too.

Cole was just asking for trouble if he got in that card game. But Cole could not stand a cheat because they always figured they were smarter than everybody else. Cole got another drink then walked over to the poker table. "Mind if I sit in?" he asked as he pulled out some money.

He lay down his first two hands while checking the cards. It was a marked deck. He asked for a new deck of cards which pissed the man in the silk shirt off. The woman in the red dress started to come beside him so he turned his cards down telling her he did not need anything right now. He won the hand. Cole continued to watch the man to the right of the man in the silk shirt. He was medium built, curly dark hair, acting drunk with beet looking eyes. He knew they were getting ready to set him up and it was not long before the dealer slipped the man a card from the bottom of the deck.

Cole got a pair of kings, he bet and asked for three cards knowing the heavyset man in the silk shirt had a pair of aces when he also took three cards. Now he guessed he would get a king and maybe a pair. He got a king and a pair of fours making him a full house. That meant the man in the silk shirt would get an ace and a pair to make him a bigger full house and beat Cole's hand. The dealer knew Cole was watching him, so that left the heavyset man in the silk shirt unobserved to pull out an ace from his sleeve. After the hand, they would discard the aces.

Cole leaned forward in his chair, while telling the big man that he must have one hell of a hand. At the same time, Cole reached for his bowie knife with his left hand. When he leaned back in the chair the bowie knife was where he wanted it. The heavyset man in the silk shirt told Cole it would cost him a thousand dollars to see his hand.

Cole said, "Mister, that is a lot of money for someone who's a cheat!" Before he got the word cheat out, Cole threw the knife into cards on the table. At the same time, he drew his gun, pointing it at the heavyset man's head.

"Tell your friend behind me to come around where you are before I blow your brains out."

The big man was sweating for he knew Cole meant it. After the other man came around in front of Cole, he asked the other men playing how many aces were in a deck because he had three aces and there were two where the bowie knife was stuck making a total of five aces.

The other players looked and sure enough there were. Cole told them the pot belonged to the losers and they could divide it however they wanted. One of the players asked Cole if all three were in on the cheating.

Cole responded, "Yes, plus the gal in the red dress." Cole told the crowd, "Drinks are on the man in the silk shirt!" and ordered him to hand over his billfold. The man's face was red with rage when he told Cole that he would not forget him.

Cole said, "If you all are smart, you'd be getting out of here before this crowd gets drunk and remembers what you did - but you do whatever you think."

They thought about it and left with the big man still running his mouth about getting Cole. Opening the billfold to pay for drinks, Cole discovered four thousand dollars inside the wallet. He handed the bartender 500 dollars and told the crowd, "drinks are free until 500 dollars is gone." He asked the bartender if there was a back door in case his crooked poker friends were waiting outside for him. The jolly, fat bartender was happy to help. He told him to go through the side door which would put him in the restaurant and to go out the restaurant side door which would put him on a side street to the hotel.

Chapter 5

The next morning, Cole went back to the restaurant for a breakfast of ham and eggs.

Ben, drinking his morning coffee, told Cole he heard about last night and they had left town without paying their bill. Grinning, Cole told Ben they had given him the money to pay it.

Cole peeled a fifty-dollar bill out and handed it to him.

Ben said, "I can't change that!"

"Oh," Cole said, "the big man told you to keep the change."

Before Ben could say anything, Cole asked about Blackjack. Ben started to answer, but was interrupted by a bunch of noise coming from the back corner of the restaurant dining room. Several women were gathered, discussing how to raise money for a new church. Cole finished his breakfast and told Ben he'd see him in a little while.

Walking back to where the women were, Cole took his hat off saying "Excuse me ladies, but I was sent here to bring this money to you." Cole handed one of the women two thousand dollars. He told them to spend it wisely.

One of women said, "Who sent you here with the money?"

Cole looked at the women and responded, "God did, Madam." He turned to leave, but then turned back to the women and said, "Oh yeah, He would like the church to have a big bell. He likes to hear the bell. You all have a good day." Cole turned to walk out of the restaurant.

It was a nice morning to walk around town with a light breeze. He ended up at the livery stable to check on Blackjack and to talk to Ben, who was in his little office when Cole walked in. He explained his problem with the three brothers chasing him for killing their brother and that's why he needed Blackjack ready to go. Cole figured since they lost his trail when it rained, it only made sense they would send out men to different towns trying to locate him. The first place they would come to in a new town was the livery stable and the saloon. He told Ben to tell them the truth, he did not want him getting involved or hurt. "Tell them I'm headed for Texas. When they see the trail is headed that way, they all should follow me and leave you alone. I need to leave in three days with Blackjack rested up. If some men come looking for me before the third day, send your helper to warn me and get Blackjack ready with my supplies. Ben, be very careful, they have 30 men riding with them."

Chapter 6

On the second day, just past noon, three men rode into town. They stopped at the livery stable and asked if a man with a big black stallion had been there. Ben showed them the stallion in the corral. The one man named Bill, giving orders to the other two men, asked Ben to sell him a fresh horse. Bill told a stocky built man in his thirties to hurry back with the rest of the men. The other man, who stayed behind with Bill, was no cowboy. He was a tall, lanky, redhead with pale skin who wore his gun low and went by the name Loco Joe; a gunfighter. While the redheaded gunslinger stared at Ben, the other man, Bill asked if he had seen the owner of the black stallion. Ben told him he had come by about an hour ago to check on the black stallion, and he was going to have a drink of whiskey before he headed for Texas, but he didn't know which saloon he had gone to.

He crossed the street to Ben's place to find out what they looked like and where they were. Ben told him they went up the street looking in saloons. Cole told Ben to tell them he saw him go into the Merry Gay saloon when they came back this way.

"Cole, one of them is Loco Joe, a gunslinger who has killed twelve men!" stated Ben. "Maybe it would be wise to ride out."

Cole paused before he spoke, "Well, I reckon not. But if something happens to me, promise me you will turn Blackjack loose. I couldn't stand the idea of one of those jerks mistreating him."

Cole headed for the Merry Gay to find a place to get his eyes adjusted to the dark. He found a table in the corner of the room and ordered a whiskey. It was not long before they walked in.

Cole yelled, "I hear you two are looking for me!"

Both reached to draw their weapons,

Cole shot Loco Joe first in the heart and the other one, Bill, in the shoulder. The room was almost emptied out when the gun smoke cleared. Cole walked over where Bill lay, kicked his gun away, and made sure Loco Joe was dead. Cole tried to tell Bill that his brother had ambushed him and he did not have any choice but to kill him. Cole turned to walk away, when someone yelled, "Watch out, he's got a gun!? Cole felt the bullet tear into his arm as he swung around to shoot Bill in the head.

Bill had a derringer stuck in his pant leg which Cole did not see. Ben was the one who yelled at Cole as he looked at his arm. It was a flesh wound, missing the bone, but it needed to be looked at by a doctor.

The doctor, an older man in his late sixties, was taking a nap because he had been up all night delivering twins. He was a short, frail man with gray hair, what hair he had. He told Cole, he would be sore, but he was a lucky man, and wrapped up his arm. Cole tossed the doctor a twenty-dollar gold coin. When the doctor told Cole he could not change the twenty dollars, Cole just smiled and told the doctor to put it on his account.

Ben had Blackjack saddled and ready to go when Cole walked into the livery.

"Remember, Ben," Cole remarked, "You overheard me talking to a cowhand about the best trail to Texas that should lead them away from here."

Chapter 7

Cole and Blackjack headed south toward the Indian Nation. He kept looking over his shoulder for signs of being followed as he pushed on. He had been riding Blackjack hard trying to lose what he knew was behind him.

Cole got tired of running, both he and Blackjack needed to rest. He came across a stream of water, with green grass for Blackjack to eat and a clump of trees where he could camp. After Cole had taken care of Blackjack by rubbing him down, he turned him loose to graze and drink. He built a small fire for coffee, ate a hot meal, rolled out his bedroll for the night. His arm was hurting more than it should. He kept his pistols close to his side as he drifted off to sleep.

The next morning, Cole was running a fever. Looking to see if Blackjack was alright, he put some wood on the coals to make some coffee and maybe cook some bacon to go with the biscuits Ben had packed for him. Cole's camp was where he could see for miles behind him so he decided to rest a couple of days. On the second night, he saw a campfire in the distance about where he had been. In the morning, he would saddle up and move on toward Texas. He thought if only it would rain maybe he could lose them. But right now, it was a game of cat and mouse and whoever made the first mistake would pay with their lives. For the next couple of days, Cole pushed Blackjack hard to stay ahead. The horse never complained, but Cole was not going to run him into ground. Cole was looking for a place to make a stand. He was getting deep into Indian Territory, it looked like his luck was running out. Up ahead, he saw riders coming his way, glancing to his right and left flank, he saw more riders. There was nothing he could do but ride head on. Cole knew what was behind him, but he had no idea who these riders were. He figured they were probably outlaws. There was no place to take cover, so he pulled Blackjack to a halt as they swarmed in on him.

One of men in back of the pack said, "Well, well, I heard you got killed at Gettysburg." The rider pushed to the front of the pack. He was hollow eyed, battle worn and a thin man, but Cole knew that voice. He was his sister's husband, Lee, who had fought for the Confederacy under General Stand Watie. Lee stared at Cole for few moments before he spoke, "Oh hell, if I kill you, my wife will never speak to me... and again it might be worth it."

"Well, Lee, you do what you think best, but the war is over," Cole replied.

"Oh yeah, why are thirty some men chasing you?"

Cole grinned and replied, "Well, you know me; trouble always finds me. I had to kill two brothers and the rest of them have been chasing me since Dodge City. I was headed for your house, but I could not bring you my problems, so I decided to head for Texas."

He studied his men and Lee said, "I cannot speak for my men, but if you need help, guess I can help since they are Jay Hawker's."

"I appreciate that, Lee, but you need to take care of my sister, she needs you."

Not listening to Cole, he ordered two of his men to get some brush to cover up the horseshoe prints and all headed for Red Rock Canyon - a perfect place for an ambush. Lee told Cole to wait until the men were a quarter of a mile from him and then hightail it south to Red Rock Canyon. Lee's men would then ambush them at there. Which was a place used by the plains Indians in the winter time.

Four hours later, Cole saw the red dust before he saw the riders coming up fast. He mounted Blackjack and heard rifle fire, galloping south toward the canyon, he stayed in their sight, but just out of rifle range. Cole entered the Red Rock Canyon, riding hard and low in the saddle. He could hear gunfire coming down from the canyon walls, and behind the riders as they entered the canyon.

Turning the big black horse around, Cole dismounted and grabbed his rifle, told Blackjack to get on down the canyon. He started firing into the men who had been chasing him. Gun smoke filled the canyon with the screams of dying men laying around on the ground. It was not long before Lee's men were looting their bodies, gathering their weapons and horses to divide up among themselves.

Lee walked over and told Cole the only way his men would help a Yankee was if they got what these men had. Afterward they dragged the bodies to a deep ravine and threw them into it. It was kill or be killed, but Cole felt sick to his stomach. The walls of the canyon were blood red with the smell of death. The next morning, six of Lee's men bid him farewell and headed south for home. The other four headed east along with Lee and Cole towards Cherokee country. Cole was finally glad to be heading home to see his family after close to five years away. He just hoped he and Luke could get along. Sometimes Luke could be a hard head with that temper of his. His sister Sarah could always handle Luke, but he and Cole always seemed to butt heads. They camped that night under some big cottonwood trees close to a running spring. Cole turned Blackjack loose to graze in the tall grass.

"Boy that sure is a beautiful horse, but what if he wants to run off or if someone tries to steal him?" Lee asked Cole.

"Oh, Blackjack's got a mind of his own of who can ride him plus he is a real good watch dog with a high spirit. It sure will be good to see Grandpa, Mary, and the rest of the family."

Lee said, "I dreamt of Sarah so much that I am going to grab her, get under the covers and not come out for a week."

Cole laughed - it felt good to be happy again.

Lee was tall, slim built, half Cherokee, with his father being a Frenchman. He was a cousin to Ruth, who was Cole's first love. Suddenly Lee's face got serious. Poking a stick in the fire he said, "You know, Cole, Ruth got married about two years ago?

Cole did not say anything for a long time. Finally, when he did, he quietly said, "Tell her that I wish her the best."

Lee studied Cole's face a while before he spoke, "Maybe I should've kept my mouth shut. but when I asked Sarah to marry me, everyone was against it, but you. Can I ask you why since we were not friends?"

Watching the fire eat up the dry wood, Cole looked up as he spoke, "Hell, Lee, Sarah loves you and you love her, it's that simple."

"Well Cole, maybe I should not tell you since Ruth is my cousin, but I think you have the right to know. Ruth has a boy."

Staring into the fire, Cole watched the flames gobble up the dry wood. Forcing himself to speak he said, "I only wish the best for Ruth, she deserves to be happy. Do not worry Lee, I will not bother her."

"You do not understand, Cole; the boy is fourteen years old and he looks like you, that is the reason her family sent her away, because her father said that she had shamed the family by having a black, Irish bastard."

Cole had a hurt, mean look on his face. "You telling me that you knew all these years that I had a son and you did not tell me after I stood up for you?"

Shaking his head, Lee said, "No, I only found out two years ago. When Ruth got married, her husband got drunk, and told everybody he had to take care of your little bastard son. I might as well tell you all of it. Ruth's father forced her to marry this man. He told her if she did not, he would take the boy to Mexico and sell him. Ruth's husband drank a lot and beat on her. I have been told that your grandpa found out, tried to get him, but Ruth's husband beat him up. With all of us fighting in the war, nobody was around to help him. Ruth just gave up when she heard you got killed."

Poking hard at the fire with a wooden stick, Cole told Lee, "It looks like someone's got a good ass whipping coming to them. We will be home in about three days if this nice weather holds up. Thanks for everything, Lee. That Kansas bunch almost had me by my balls."

Chapter 8

Three days later, around three o'clock, Cole and Lee rode up to the ranch. The house was a big wooden frame house, a little bigger than most, because so many people lived in it. There was Grandpa, Mary, Sarah, Lee and their two children. Down by the barn was the bunkhouse and the corral where Cole broke a lot of wild horses when he was growing up.

The house had a porch which covered most of the front of the house where a person could sit and watch the sunset. What should have been a happy day, since Cole and Lee were home from the war, turned out to be a sad day. Ruth had been raped and murdered at her house the day before while her husband was in town getting drunk. Ruth's son, Sam, was working at a ranch close by. He found her that evening, still alive. She told him three men had ridden in looking for money. When they could not find any money, they raped her and cut her up with a knife, leaving her for dead. She lived long enough to tell Sam what they looked like and that she heard them talk about going to Colorado. Cole's grandpa and three men from the Indian Police, Light Horse Company out of Tahlequah, took off after the men early that morning. Light Horse Company was composed of a captain, lieutenant and 24 horsemen. Their duty was to pursue and arrest all fugitives from justice and turn them over to the Indian Courts for trial and punishment. The Cherokee got the name Light Horse' from the Revolutionary War hero, General Henry Lee, who was called Light Horse Harry due to his rapid cavalry movements. General Lee was Robert E. Lee's father. The Cherokee justice for rape, the first time, was 50 lashes on the bare back, and the left ear cut off close to head. The 2nd time was 100 lashes and the other ear cut off. The third time was death by hanging in Tahlequah. Some of Light Horse's men were black and white men who lived with the Cherokee.

Sarah and Mary were cooking supper while Cole tended to Blackjack. He was giving him a good rub down and talking to him. He did not notice Sam until he heard a noise behind him. Turning around he looked into the sad eyes of a boy trying to be a man. Sam was tall and skinny with his mother's features, but Cole could see himself also. His words were bitter and angry toward Cole.

"You do not care enough about my mother to go after those men."

"Sam, I can cover more miles if I let Blackjack rest until morning. I promise you I will go after them them. I loved your mother and I did not know about you until a couple of days ago.

"I want to go with you, to get them!" Sam insisted.

"No, Sam, me and Blackjack will have to move fast. You stay here with Lee and see to it your mother gets a proper funeral. Where is your stepfather?"

Sam replied, "The sonofabitch never came home, he's laying up in Tahlequah, drunk. He is a piece of crap like my mother's dad. That why Grandpa went with the police - if he stayed, he would have killed my stepfather. He told me to stay here, watch after the women. Cole, he told me all about you. He and mother heard you got killed, mother was never the same after that. She told me a part of her died, the only thing that kept her going was me."

Sam was patting Blackjack as he continued talking, not aware of the horse's movement until Blackjack snorted and pounded his hoof.

Cole said, "That is his way of telling you he likes you. Talk to him. I need to go talk to Lee, why don't you stay with Blackjack?"

Opening the front door, Cole noticed everyone sitting around the kitchen table drinking coffee and talking about Ruth. He told no one in particular that he would be heading out in the morning to catch up with the ones chasing Ruth's killers. He also stated that right now he wanted Lee to loan him a horse and that he wanted Blackjack to rest while he took care of some business in town.

"What was Ruth's husband's name and where can I find him?" Cole asked Mary. "He will not beat on Sam again."

Mary replied, "His name is Roy Bee, but watch out, he's got two guys to help him."

Lee said, "I will go with you."

Cole replied, "No, I thank you, but you need to stay with Sarah, she needs you. Sam's a fine boy, I just wish Ruth was alive, so I could tell her."

Cole rode into town on a red sorrel horse looking for Roy Bee. The whole town knew why he had come because Roy Bee had been running his mouth about killing Cole if he came looking for him. There was only one saloon, the last building on the right, in this small town. About a block from the saloon, Cole dismounted the horse, in case they were trying to ambush him. He saw someone run into the saloon. Their plan was probably to shoot him as soon as he walked in the door. It would be smarter to come in the back door to see what he was up against. Cole walked in behind the three men with their guns aimed at the front door.

"You looking for me!" Cole barked.

Two of the men swirled around to fire their guns, but Cole was too fast for them. Both hit the floor dead. Cole turned his gun toward the third man, but the man tossed his gun aside.

Cole glared at him. "Bet you're that yellow-bellied coward, Roy Bee," Cole said as he took off his guns and tossed them on a table. Walking up to Roy with his fists clenched, he hit him across the jaw with his right, then followed with a left that broke Roy's nose, knocking him to the bar floor. As he rolled across the bar floor, Roy Bee jumped up grabbed a gun, but before he could fire, Cole threw his bowie knife, sticking him in his gut. He watched as Roy fell to the floor.

Cole remarked, "I bet you will not be beating on any more women or kids now, you sonofabitch!" Cole pulled the knife out and wiped the blood off on Roy's shirt. Glancing around the bar, he put his Bowie away, reached for his two navy Colt pistols, and headed for the door.

Sam was waiting for him in the barn with Blackjack when he rode in to turn the horse loose in the corral. Cole was tired, but he needed to talk to Sam before he left at daybreak to catch up with his grandpa and the posse.

"I want you, Sam, to move in with Mary, help Lee around here and mind Sarah until I get back. They said you were welcome to stay. I don't know when I will be back, but I will be back, and then you and me can get better acquainted. But right now, I need to go after Ruth's killers."

Sam nodded his head in agreement, "Mom said that I get the love of horses after you, is that right?"

Cole replied, "I do love to be around horses, just ask Blackjack if I do."

Sam was astonished when Blackjack nodded his head up and down, snorted and pounded his hoofs. Grinning, Cole told Sam it was the love that Blackjack and he shared a special bond because of how they treated and respected each other, that's what makes a great horse. "It's late and I always like the fresh smell of hay so I am going to bed down here in barn tonight."

Sam said, "Me too, if you do not mind."

"No, I would like the company," Cole said as he rolled out his bedroll, "But do you have a blanket?"

"Yeah, I sleep here when I stay over and it's a nice night to sleep out."

Cole always thought of Ruth when he smelled fresh hay. Things might have been different if Ruth's father had given Cole a chance and not been so prejudice.

Chapter 9

The next morning Cole got up at daybreak and went up to the ranch house.

Sarah and Mary were both fixing breakfast. Mary fried the bacon and eggs as Sarah made the coffee.

Cole sat down at the table and realized he had not asked about his brother, Luke. Sarah told him the last time she heard from Luke, that he had bought a ranch in Texas. Cole asked Sarah if she minded if Sam stayed with her since he was going after Ruth's killers.

"No, Sam is a good boy, but what is Roy Bee going to say about it when he sobers up?" Sarah replied.

Mary spoke up, "I will kill the "sonofabitch if he thinks that he can use Sam like a slave!?

"Well, Mary, that is going to be hard to do since he is already dead along with his two friends. Ruth told Sam about me, I guess everyone knew but me," Cole said.

Mary poured Cole some coffee, while his sister Sarah fixed him a plate of food.

About that time, Lee walked into the kitchen. Cole asked him if he would mind Sam staying with them until he got back. Glancing over toward Cole eating, Lee told him that Sam had just as much right to be here as he did, and besides he needed the help, getting the ranch back in shape.

"Well, I better get to riding before the sun gets too high," Cole said. "I'm going to cut over to Kansas, head west to Fort Morgan, and then north to Denver."

Cole shook Lee's hand and thanked him again, kissed Mary and Sarah each on their cheek, and went to the barn to saddle Blackjack. After he got him ready, he went to open the barn door, and took one last look at Sam sleeping. Blackjack had a different idea - he walked over where Sam was sleeping and with his big head pushed Sam awake. Sam looked confused at first, grabbed at Blackjack's mane, but learning who it was, he jumped up and hugged his big black neck.

Cole shook his head, "I was going let you sleep. Guess Blackjack wanted to tell you goodbye. That means he likes you. You listen to Lee; I will be back."

Chapter 10

The first couple days they made good time. Cole was back in Kansas when it started raining hard, so he held up until the rain blew over, then he pushed on west. A couple of weeks later, he arrived at Fort Morgan, both him and Blackjack were worn out and there was no place to rest up. Cole rode on into town, not far from the fort. Cole was glad to see the blacksmith still open and he put the saddle in the tack room, keeping his saddle bags. Telling the blonde headed young boy to give his horse a double order of oats and a good rubdown, he flipped him a silver dollar.

He checked in at the hotel, got a good hot bath, a change of clothing and, noticing the saloon was still open, decided to get a drink of whiskey. Cole had almost finished his second drink, while standing at the end of bar, when three men walked in and ordered a bottle of whiskey to go.

The bartender gave them a dirty look, and said, "We don't serve no Indians here!"

One of men said, "We are lawmen from Indian Territory tracking three men who raped and murdered a woman."

Cole glanced around the room and saw two men acting nervous. The men stood up, pulling out their guns, when one of them said, "We did not know it was a crime to kill an Indian - and three more won't matter!"

"Hey, you boys, I got a question," Cole said and then continued, "How are you going to shoot them in the back, without me shooting you?"

Both men swung around toward the end of bar to gun Cole down, but Cole was too fast for them. Both men fell across chairs and onto the dirt floor. One of them, who was hit in the hip, was still alive. The other man was dead, shot in the heart. Cole kept his guns pointed, one at the bartender, the other at the man on the floor. He asked the three Indian lawmen to cover the crowd and walking over, he put his boot on the fresh wound of the man he had shot. Cole mashed down as the man screamed in pain. Cole told him the Indian woman they killed was his woman and if he wanted to live to see Cherokee country again, he'd better tell where the third man was, or he would take him and skin him alive, the Indian way. The man screamed out that the third man had left them two days ago and was heading up along the South Plate River in Colorado. The man's curly blond hair was wet with sweat, begging for his life.

"What did the sonofabitch look like and what was his name?" yelled Cole.

Hesitating the man said, "Why should I tell you? What do I get?"

Cole grabbed him by the collar, reached down and pulled out his bowie knife and stuck it to his face. "You get to live a little longer and I will not skin you."

The man's face was pale with sweat. "It was not my idea to rape and kill her. Johnny Bell is his name. He is about your height, dark hair, with a scar on his right arm from the wrist all the way to his elbow."

"You better be telling me the truth or I will come for you!" Cole told him with an icy stare.

One of Indian lawmen said they had been tracking horses and one set of tracks headed up that way. The old man, who was riding with the lawmen, took off after him. The Indian lawmen could not go up that way because it was out of their jurisdiction, so they followed these two here. With everybody's attention on Cole and the Indian lawmen, the bartender slowly reached for a sawed-off shotgun behind the bar. Suddenly, Cole pointed his Colt at him and said, "If you want see what hell looks like, go ahead, pull it. I will blow a hole in that fat belly of yours." The big bartender raised his hands up. One of Indian lawmen went behind the bar and took the shotgun.

"Did I hear you say drinks on the house, or did I not?" Cole asked the big sweating bartender. "First, one of you men go for the sheriff and the doctor, while me and my friends have a bottle of whiskey over there at the back table, if you are buying Mr. Bartender."

Two of the Indian lawmen dragged the man Cole shot over to the back table to wait for the doctor and kept an eye on him. The sheriff walked in with a deputy who carried a shotgun. The sheriff was a man in his thirties, heavyset with long brown hair and a mustache. Acting nervous he approached the back table. He demanded to know what was going on.

Cole explained what happened and one of the Indian lawmen showed him the papers. The sheriff tossed the papers on the floor, "We do not honor no papers from the Indian Nations, or let them drink with us." The sheriff glanced at Cole, "Mister, you are in bad company, I give you three seconds to leave this table."

Cole rose from his chair, "The only bad company here is you, Sheriff."

"Before my deputy blows you to kingdom come, tell me your name so we can put it on your headstone!" the sheriff yelled.

"Well, Sheriff, I would not worry about it, because you will be as dead as me, but if it makes you happy, the name's Cole Turley."

The sheriff's face turned pale, his fingers trembling he asked, the same Cole Turley them brothers in Dodge City are looking to kill?"

"That's right, but they are not looking anymore, they found me." Without taking his eyes off the sheriff, he said to the three Indian lawmen, "If that deputy gets lucky, kill him for me."

The sheriff threw up his hands, "Wait, - we don't want to see anybody get killed over a misunderstanding. It's a federal crime, take your prisoner to the fort to get treated, it's their problem not mine."

Cole gave the sheriff a cold icy death stare, "Just as soon as we finish our bottle of whiskey. Get us our free drink the bartender promised us." Cole glanced over at the heavyset bartender, "That's what you promised us, right?"

Sweat was pouring off the bartender as he nodded his head in agreement. When someone pushed Cole, he pushed back twice as hard, to let them know if they were going to mess with him, they would pay for it.

"Well, Sheriff, I guess we do not need you after all. They are going to take their prisoner to the fort and I am going after the third man in the morning.

Anxiously, the sheriff and the deputy left the saloon.

Cole told the Indian lawman if they had any more trouble, to send one of them to get him at the hotel. If he didn't hear from them, he would figure everything was alright and he would then head after his grandpa and the third person.

The next morning after he had breakfast, he paid his hotel bill. Cole headed for the livery stable to check on Blackjack and to also see if the man had a mule for sale.

His last stop was to the store to get supplies and a fur coat. Cole's mother was part Ute and growing up, he had spent a lot of summers and some winters visiting his grandparents in the nearby Medicine Bow Mountains in the Yampa Valley, along the White River, a special place for Utes who bred and raced their prized horses for generations. The Ute men wore buckskin shirts, breech cloth with leather leggings. They were outstanding horsemen. Ute women wore long dresses made of deerskin. Each spring, an important ceremony, lasting four days called the Bear Dance was held to awake the bear from its winter sleep, so the bear could lead them to food. Ute never hunted bears. The Ute were proud people that knew the land and the weather. Cole learned a storm could blow in anytime without too much warning. Cole packed the mule down with supplies, saddled up Blackjack, and headed for the mountains in search of his grandpa and a fellow named Johnny Bell.

Chapter 11

During the first week, Cole made good time without any trouble. But during the second week, he ran into some desperate miners who wanted his supplies. He told the three miners, he would feed them and give them enough food to make it to the fort. But Cole knew the miners wanted everything he had and they did not mind killing him to get it.

The bigger miner, with a full beard and greased black hair tried to get Cole's attention while the other two miners pulled out their pistols.

Cole jumped behind a tree as tour shots rang out. The big bearded miner ran at Cole firing his revolver. Cole pulled his Navy Colts and dropped the big miner with one shot. At the same time, the other two men rushed him from the other direction. Cole calmly stepped out from behind the tree and dropped both of them - they were dead before they hit the ground.

Cole was tired of killing but trouble always seemed to find him. He knew the closer he got to where gold was, people who had come without provisions or ran out would be very desperate to take what he had brought with him. Most of these miners did not Know how bad the winters could be. Cole had brought his mother's people gifts, for he had not seen them before the Civil War had started.

He decided it would be wise to find them first before he went looking for his grandpa and this fellow named Johnny Bell. The last time he heard, they were around Fort Lupton, an independent trading post built by Lancaster Lupton, which was the first permanent settlement in northern Colorado. But the Ute people were not the kind to stay in one place, especially with prospectors trampling all over their land looking for gold. The gold seekers tried to follow an old Ute trail across the continental divide, only to be killed or driven back. The Lost Mine of Dead Man Gulch was another place littered with prospectors' bones.

Cole headed Blackjack toward the old trading post. Maybe it he was lucky, he would find them or someone who knew their whereabouts.

He arrived at the trading post late one night and found a place to bed down outside the gates after he took care of Blackjack and the mule. It was too late for a hot meal and he was tired so he chewed on some beef jerky.

Cole saw an Indian camp in the distance and figured he would check it out in morning.

Right now he needed some sleep.

Chapter 12

Early the next morning, Blackjack started snorting and pounding his hoofs letting Cole know that something was outside the camp. Cole watched a pair of hands put a rope around Blackjack's neck to lead him away.

Holding his Colt, Cole pretended to be asleep.

A young Ute Indian tried to pull Blackjack away from the camp. Cole whistled and the big black stallion reared up causing the young Ute to fall on the ground. Before he could get up, Cole grabbed a hold of him. Kicking and screaming the boy tried to get loose, but Cole knew enough of Ute language to calm him down. Cole told the boy if he didn't run, he would turn him loose. The boy agreed and Cole let go. Cole motioned the boy over to where he left some dry wood to build a campfire. The Ute boy watched Cole get the fire going to brew some coffee. Cole pulled out a candy stick from his saddle bag and tossed it to the young boy. He stared at Cole, too proud to accept it.

Cole was trying to ask him if he knew Red Hand, explaining he was his grandson and was looking for him. The Ute boy, using his hands, told him when the sun came up, he would be back. Cole whistled for Blackjack to bring the boy's rope still around his big black neck. Cole motioned to the boy to take his rope. He patted the big stallion and removed his rope. As quick as he came, the boy was gone.

Daylight came and the Ute boy brought an older Ute Indian to the camp. Cole poured himself another cup of coffee. Blackjack was grazing a short distance away from the camp.

The older Indian stopped to admire the black stallion. With broken English he asked Cole what he wanted. Cole offered him and the boy some coffee and motioned for them to sit with him. The older Ute sat down and kept his eyes on Cole while he drank his coffee. Cole asked him about Red Hand. He could tell by his expression that he knew him. Cole did not know it he was talking to a friend or foe of his grandfather. Looking for an expression on the Indian's face, he told him that Red Hand was his grandfather. Slapping his chest, he told Cole that Tall Tree was his name. Cole understood how he came by his name for the Indian was tall and slim. Tall Tree motioned for the boy to leave and asked Cole for more coffee all the while keeping his eyes on Cole. Blackjack walked over where Cole was and, with his cold nose, pushed at Cole. Reaching in his pocket, Cole pulled out a lump of sugar and gave it to him. Blackjack walked back over to edge of camp and started grazing the green grass.

The sun was getting high in the sky when he noticed a group of Indians coming toward his camp. He kept one eye on Tall Tree and the other on the Indians coming. His grandmother was following behind the rest.

She looked tired, frail and skinny, but had a big smile on her face. She stretched out her arms to hug him. Cole hugged her and talked as much Ute language as he could remember. Glancing around, he asked her where grandfather was.

With pain in her eyes and her voice trembling, she told Cole he had been killed by Arapahos down at South Park Way of the Platte Canyon almost a year before. Cole got his grandmother some coffee, sat her down on his bedroll with his saddle behind it. She introduced Cole to some of his kin. Everyone was friendly except a young brave in his twenties with a muscular body and long black hair by the name of Lone Wolf. Cole overlooked his rude manners and fetched his grandmother the gifts that he had brought on the mule. He gave her a pretty purple wool coat to keep her warm along with a sack of flour, a bag of coffee and a box of candy. Cole put aside his gifts for his grandfather, some tobacco and a beautiful Bowie knife, and tossed the kids some candy sticks.

Cole was leaning against a cottonwood tree, talking to his grandmother, when the young buck threw a knife at the tree, close to his head. Cole reached over and pulled the knife out and threw it where it stuck in ground by the buck's right foot. his cousin, the young buck, had challenged Cole to a fight and Cole had accepted. The young buck grabbed the knife and came at Cole with a big grin on his face. Cole took his hat, slapped him across his eyes, and at the same time grabbed his arm with the knife, elbowing him in his side. He was strong, but Cole managed to get the knife from him, held it to his throat and asked him to give or he would ram that knife down his throat. He dropped his hands as a sign he gave up.

Cole stayed a few days with his grandmother for they both knew it would be the last time they would see each other. Cole went to the fort to get more supplies for her before he headed out. At the trading post, Cole overheard two men talking about an old man who had just come from Indian territory and had struck it rich, when he was not even looking for gold, down by Steamboat Springs. It was a long shot and with the trail cold, it was like finding a needle in the haystack. But Cole did not have any choice, it was the only lead he had. As soon as he took care of his grandmother, making sure she had everything she needed, he would head south. He gave some tobacco to Tall Tree and because he was his grandfather's best friend, he would look after his grandmother, this he knew. But he debated giving Lone Wolf the Bowie knife. His grandmother told him, Lone Wolf was jealous of him, because his grandfather had always bragged on Cole.

Leaving the Indian camp, Cole hugged his grandmother goodbye. He stopped beside Lone Wolf, sticking out his hand in friendship.

Lone Wolf took his hand, shook it, and smiled.

Cole reached for the bowie knife, cut his hand, and gave the knife to Lone Wolf who did the same, and the two joined their hands together.

Lone Wolf handed Cole the knife back. Cole told him to keep it as a sign of them being blood brothers. Cole asked him to look after their grandmother for the Ute days of roaming the country were few because the white man wanted the land.

Cole stopped by the trading post to get more supplies before he headed out. The short, bald man with whiskers, who ran the trading post, asked Cole what happened to all the supplies he had sold him. He glared at the storekeeper then watched the men at the table nearby listening for his answer. Cole replied that two white men had robbed him and they would have gotten his horse and mule, also, if the Ute Indians had not come by and scared them off. Cole told him that he was going after them to get his supplies back. One of the men at the table, a tall man with blond hair and a scar over his left eye, wearing a red shirt, said, "That's funny, I saw your horse at the Indian camp for a long time."

Cole glared and then smiled, "Yeah, that was me. I thought maybe I could hire a couple of them to track the two men. Hey, maybe one of you might be interested in the job. I cannot pay, but I will split the supplies they took from me with you."

Cole saddled up the mule with the supplies and headed south on the trail. He told Blackjack about the good bluff that he told the men at the store. With blue clouds hanging low overhead and the sun bright in the sky, Cole headed for the rampa Valley. Steamboat Springs lies against the western ridge of the Continental Divide with the Yampa River flowing through the town. Meeting up with the Green River downstream, Steamboat had several natural hot springs in the area for an aching body to soak in. But gold had been discovered at Han's Peak by the man from Indian Nations so Cole headed toward it.

Cole came upon a small mining camp, about dusk, on the trail to Han's Peak. It looked like most of the miners were panning for gold in the stream running down the mountain. Someone must have found gold in the creek bed to have this many miners here.

Glancing around the camp, he saw a wagon off to the side with a woman and two small children playing with a dog. He motioned Blackjack in that direction. Stopping by the wagon, he tipped his hat and asked, "Madam, would it be alright if I camped over by that tree?"

The woman looked older than she was, a little heavy with red hair and a bonnet to block out the sun. She spoke with a quick tone, "don't own the land, camp anywhere you want?"

"Thank you, madam, do you mind if I give your two children a stick of candy, because it will just go to waste?"

The mention of candy got the two kids' attention and Cole did not wait for an answer. Reaching into his saddle bag, he pulled out two sticks of candy. "Now wait until after supper," he said as he handed the candy to them.

He unsaddled Blackjack, laid out his bedroll, and built a campfire. Cole led the big black stallion down to the creek with two canteens to fill. While the horse drank some water, Cole filled the canteens and noticed a shiny piece of rock laying at bottom of the creek. Picking it up, he saw that it was gold.

Looking around he did not notice anyone. He stuck it in his front pocket. Leading the big stallion back up to the camp, he got out a brush to brush him.

He heard someone behind him as he twirled around to see the woman's husband coming into his camp. "Hey, I want apologize for my wife. To tell you the truth, she was scared. We're on our way to California. When we heard about the gold strike, we decided to try our luck at it before we moved on. My wife would like to make up for her bad manners by inviting you to supper. We are sorry, but all we got is beans and no coffee. My name is Brown, my friends call me Henry."

"Well Henry, my name is Cole Turley and if it does not offend you, I got some coffee to share with the supper."

Henry, a man in his forties with thin hair, not too tall, and was built like someone who was used to hard work.

He asked if he was the same Cole Turley who was a gunfighter.

Cole handed Henry the bag of coffee and asked if it made a difference.

"No, it does not make any difference, you are welcome in my camp. You have treated my family good and I stuck my nose in your affairs. Now I need to apologize for my bad manners. Let's go and eat."

After they had eaten, the kids were put to bed and Henry's wife, Sue, cleaned up the dishes. Henry and Cole sat by the fire just talking. Cole noticed Henry kept reaching for his front pocket.

"Did you lose something?" Cole asked him.

"No, I just keep reaching for my tobacco for my pipe but it is all gone."

Cole told him, "it's none of my business but you need to get your family out of here before the weather gets bad. I know how bad it can get."

Henry nodded his head in agreement, "I'm a farmer, and I figured to find some gold, buy supplies, and get out of here."

Cole reached into his pant leg pocket, pulled out a small bag of tobacco, and tossed it to Henry.

A blank expression was on Henry's face as he held it in his rough hands. Finally, he said, "I did not know you smoked."

Cole answered, I do not smoke, it was a gift for my grandfather, Red Hand - Chief of the Ute northern tribe."

Henry asked, "Are you are telling me that you are an Indian?"

"Yeah, that's about the size of it - but only part Indian, the other is Irish and black."

"Well, no matter what your race, It's a gift for your grandfather."

"My grandfather, Red Hand, will not mind, he was killed sometime back. Now I'm looking for my Irish grandfather who is trailing a cold blooded killer, a man by the name of Johnny Bell." Cole watched Henry toss the bag of tobacco around in his hand. "Are you debating smoking the tobacco of an Indian or giving it back to me?" Cole asked him.

"No, what I am wondering is why are you trying to upset me"

Cole smiled, "I am not trying to upset you - just trying to figure out what kind of man you are, Henry."

"I am the kind of man who is going to enjoy smoking my pipe again."

Cole stood up and said, "Better get some sleep. Thanks for supper."

Chapter 13

Morning came early for it seemed like Cole just closed his eyes. It wasn't long before Cole was poking at the campfire. soon after, Henry dropped by.

"Cole, you forgot your coffee last night."

"No, left it for you, besides I got more."

Puzzled, Henry told him, "Well, at least drink a cup of coffee before you head out."

Both walked back over to Henry's camp, to drink some coffee after Sue brewed it. Cole eyed Henry to see how he would take being told again that he needed to get his family out before the winter settled in and they ran out supplies.

Henry did not look up, as Cole told him the only chance his family had was it he found some gold to buy supplies, because they were almost out. Henry told Cole the only reason they came up here was they were broke and needed money for supplies. "Hell, I'm a farmer trying to get to California."

Taking a sip of coffee, Cole reached in his front pocket, pulled out the piece of gold, and tossed it to Henry and told him he could have it. He thought it was just a small pocket of gold, but if he was right, it would be worth the time. But by no means should they let anyone know they found gold. It was important for his family to keep it quiet or people would rob them. After three days of panning for gold, Cole was right, they had roughly four hundred dollars and it was time to leave. They said their goodbyes and Cole told them again to buy enough supplies at different places so people would not know how much gold they had.

Cole saddled up Blackjack, packed down the mule, and headed for Han's Peak to look for his grandfather. Traveling up the steep slope was slow going and Cole did not know if his grandfather was up there, but he had to find out. It was noontime when Cole stopped to rest Blackjack and the mule while he chewed on some beef jerky, admiring the view down below in the valley. Sometime tomorrow he should reach Han's Peak.

About four in the afternoon, Cole arrived at a small trading post with a couple of horses out front. Walking in, he noticed two men sitting at a table drinking out of a jug. He made his way over to the counter where a heavyset man with a full beard, wearing a red flannel shirt was standing. Cole asked if he knew the whereabouts of a mine which was owned by an old Irish man name of Turley.

The heavyset man laughed and said, "Do you think if I knew that, I would be here? I will tell where the cabin is for a dollar.

Cole told him he needed some coffee and flour. After he paid him, he grabbed the heavyset man by the collar, pulled out his Navy Colt, and pointed it at his head.

"Now you better be telling me the truth or I will be back to get my dollar plus interest."

Sweat poured off the heavyset man; he looked at Cole and said, "That old man will shoot anyone that comes close to the house.

"Well, I'm not anybody; I'm his grandson, Cole Turley!"

When the two men heard his name, they got up and headed out the door. The old man's house was about six miles up the mountain so Cole decided to wait until morning before heading up there so his grandfather could see him clearly in the daylight and be able to recognize him. The next morning, Cole arrived at his grandfather's cabin, but the old man was not around, but Cole knew it was his grandfather's place with his personal items laying in the cabin. There was nothing to do but wait for his grandfather's return. He took Blackjack and the mule to the barn, unsaddled the two, turned Blackjack loose in the field, and put the mule in the corral. The cabin had a porch facing a beautiful view of the valley below. Between the cabin and barn was a large deep hole that looked like someone was digging a water well, which made sense, since there was no water close by. Inside the cabin was a big fireplace.

Outside in the back was an outhouse close to a big ravine. Cole wondered how his grandfather ended up here, when he was tracking a killer.

Just past sundown, he heard the mule making noise. Thinking it was his grandfather or a mountain lion after the mule, he grabbed his rifle and went to the barn. As he opened the barn door, someone hit him on the head.

Jumping up, he made out shadows of three men. Cole had dropped his rifle when they hit him. The big heavyset man from the trading post ran at Cole, but Cole was too fast, and he hit the big man across the face, sending him rolling on the ground. The other two came at him; they were the two men drinking from the jug at the trading post. Cole picked up a wooden plank. hit the bigger one across the head. By this time, the heavyset man had gotten back up to help the other two. While the two grabbed Cole's arm, the heavyset man stuck a knife into Cole's ribcage. Cole dropped to his knees struggling to not pass out. The last thing Cole remembered was a smell of perfume before someone hit him on his head, knocking him out. Dragging Cole over to the big hole, they threw him down the shaft. The fall should have killed him, but Cole's spurs dug into the side wall, slowing down his fall. When Cole woke up, his body was wet from blood and the water at the bottom of the pit. Reaching in his pocket, he pulled out a handkerchief and poked it into the knife wound, which stopped the bleeding for the time being. He pulled himself over to the bank, close to the walls of the pit where he noticed the body of a man. Striking a match, he saw the face of his grandfather. He remembered his grandfather always carried a Bowie knife in his right leg. Cole dug a shallow grave for his grandfather and promised him he'd get him out of the water grave and get justice for his him. He tried several times to climb out but each time he fell back in the dark pit. He knew his time was running out but he had to remain calm to figure a way out.

Throwing a piece of handkerchief down the bank into a shallow stream, he noticed how fast it carried it out of sight. The water was going somewhere - maybe to the ravine behind the cabin. Cole pulled himself over where the water disappeared under a rock and started digging with his Bowie knife making a tunnel. The ground was wet and for the most part easy digging until he got into some rocks.

On the fourth day, his spirits were down and his hands were bleeding. He had been digging day and night. In the tunnel, he smelled a foul smell. Taking the Bowie knife, he dug some more, and finally saw a light shining through a small hole in the earth.

Thinking he had found the ravine, he dug the hole larger. Cole was surprised to see a big cave. The stream of water flowed out the mouth of the cave. The smell was stronger and Cole had a good idea what it was. He had dug himself into a bear den, but not just any bear, the den of a grizzly bear. Cole did not see the bear, but he knew enough about them to know the bear would smell the blood and come after him. His Ute grandfather, Red Hand, taught him about bears. His only chance was to get out of bear's den as fast as he could. Cole staggered toward the opening of the cave as quietly as he could. he kept looking for the bear. He then noticed the shiny wall of gold.

Reaching out, he grabbed several small rocks of gold and put them in his pockets. He heard the bear before he saw him. It was the biggest bear he had ever seen. Cole dove for the entrance of the cave and stepping out, he tried to turn on the narrow ledge, but tripped and rolled down a steep slope. He caught hold of a small tree with his legs and ended up hanging off the side of the mountain. With all his strength, Cole pulled himself up to a place he could rest his body. Sometime later, he climbed up a little, where he found a flat ridge leading around the mountain. Cole's knife wound was bleeding again. If he did not get the wound to stop bleeding and find warm shelter, he was in big trouble.

Chapter 4

Cole was running a high fever when he stumbled into the Indian hunting camp that night. Wet with sweat, Cole looked up into the eyes of Lone Wolf tending to his knife wound. Close by were natural hot springs to help with his fever and knife wound. Cole was fortunate that Lone Wolf and others had decided to hunt around the Red Mountain Pass in the San Juan Mountains. Cole lost track of time and how far he had walked looking for help. He stayed with Lone Wolf for three months recovering from his wound. His thoughts drifted between Blackjack and his revenge for the killing of his grandfather. He could not get that smell of perfume out of his head, for whoever knocked him in head, also, helped kill his grandfather.

The day he left Lone Wolf's winter camp, Lone Wolf gave him a horse, a gun and the Bowie knife that Cole had given him. Cole promised if he could, he would return them.

Lone Wolf handed him a bag with the gold rocks inside. Cole had forgotten about the gold, but nothing else mattered to him, just getting revenge was all that mattered. Cole headed back up to Han's Peak where the trading post was.

Chapter 15

Cole arrived around noon, and watched the trading post for the right time to attack. He waited three hours before he saw the two riders ride up to the trading post. It was the same two who had tried to kill him. Cole waited in the trees until they had drunk some. He was going up against three men, he needed some odds in his favor.

Dusk came and Cole moved toward the trading post. Surprise was on his side, for he had stopped along the way and picked up a rifle and some ammunition. Now it was time for the showdown. Glancing inside, he noticed the two cowboys sitting at a table, but the heavyset bartender and owner was nowhere to be seen. A few minutes later, the bartender came out of the back room, followed by a most beautiful black woman. Cole noticed the heavyset man was without any weapon. He walked halfway across the room grinning at the two cowboys. It was time for Cole to make his move on them. As soon as he got in the door, the two cowboys stood up to shoot, but Cole dropped them both. The heavyset man looked on in terror, begging Cole not to kill him. He would give Cole all his gold. Cole was not watching the black girl when she picked up a gun and fired. Cole threw the Bowie knife, sticking the heavyset man in the stomach.

That's when he heard the cowboy falling behind him as dead as his partner was. Cole walked over to the heavyset man, bleeding, but still alive. He jerked his bowie knife out, stuck it to his neck, and told him he would skin him alive if he did not tell him who killed his grandfather.

"Them two killed him. Johnny Bell paid them. He also paid us to kill you!"

Cole walked over to make sure the two cowboys were dead.

The black woman screamed, "I will help you, like you helped my folks." She stuck a shotgun up to heavyset man's head, pulling both triggers, scattering his brains all over the wall and herself. Watching in dismay, Cole took the shotgun from her hands. Trembling and sobbing, she repeated over and over that he had killed her folks and raped her. Cole told her to go wash up and get her belongings because they needed to go before someone showed up. While she was doing that, Cole robbed the bodies of money, found the heavyset man's safe, and took the gold he had and supplies they would need, making it look like someone came in and robbed them.

Cole grabbed a big heavy fur coat, wrapped the black woman in it. The only place he knew to go this time of night was his grandfather's place. He only hoped squatters had not moved into the place. Leaving the trading post, it started to snow heavily. With the temperature dropping, thinking about the two horses out front of the trading post, he stopped to turn them loose.

Heading up the mountain, the black woman hung on behind him. She asked Cole why not take one or both horses instead of turning them loose. He informed her that horses had a brand on them and by turning them loose, they would wander downhill, making it look like that was the direction the killers took.

"Besides, we are going to have to come up with a story as to why you are with me," Cole said.

"That's easy; you brought me from the trading post, when you came up here to your grandfather's place. You wanted a woman to keep you warm."

Cole said, "Speaking of warm, I should have gotten me a big coat."

She reached up, threw the coat over his shoulders, and pulled herself into him. Cole could feel her hot body against his back. "Guess I should ask your name if we are going to share a coat."

"Name is Jill Smith," the beautiful black woman told him, snuggling up to him more.

Arriving at the cabin, Cole was surprised no one was living there until Jill asked him if this was Turley's cabin because it was rumored to be haunted. A couple of people tried to live here, but kept hearing voices and felt like something was telling them to leave. Cole pushed the heavy door open with Jill close behind him.

He lit some candles his grandfather kept hidden. There still was a lot of firewood in the cabin so Cole built a fire, brought in the supplies, and told Jill to stay in cabin while he put the horse in the barn.

"If you don't mind, I will go with you to the barn," demanded the woman.

Cole laughed, "Come on if you want to freeze your ass off."

After they came back in, Cole fixed a bed of buffalo hides and one big bear hide for her to sleep on by the fireplace, telling Jill to get a good night's sleep.

"I'll be in the supply room if you need anything," he told her.

Jill nervously asked as her big brown eyes got wide with excitement, "Why not sleep with me? This place is spooky."

Cole replied, "I have not been with a woman in a long time. I might not be any better than the man who raped you."

Jill stood up and started taking her clothing off. "I like to sleep naked, how about you?"

Cole stared at her big breasts, firm butt and long legs. She had long dark hair and a cream color to her skin. Yeah, she was a beautiful woman alright. He stripped off his clothing and slipped in next to her. Their bodies touched with a burning hot desire, their lips pressed against each other. Jill had a hot passion for Cole the minute she saw him, maybe it was the way he handled himself. All she knew was she had a strong sexual desire.

The next morning, Jill got up early, dressed, put on a pot of coffee, and began to fix breakfast. The smell of bacon woke Cole up.

Jill asked him, "How do you like your coffee?"

Cole told her, "Black and strong."

Jill smiled and said, "You better like it that way!"

Finishing breakfast, Cole asked her if she'd be alright by herself while he went looking for his black stallion. Snow had stopped during the night and he wanted to check around and see if he could find Blackjack before it started snowing again. He gave her a pistol, told her to fire two shots if she needed him. He would not be far away. Jill was scared to stay behind but all Cole could talk about was that damn stallion and getting his grandfather's killer. She knew until he got those two things out of his system, she would not have a chance with him.

Cole found signs of a large herd of wild horses in the area sometime back. All he could do was wait until the herd came back to see if his stallion was with them. Returning to the cabin, he glanced over at the pit where his grandfather was buried. He did not mention it to anybody, hoping someone would slip up and brag about it. The sun was getting low in the sky. He looked around before going in the cabin.

Jill was fixing supper; he sat down at the table. She came up behind him when he smelled the perfume, the same perfume he had smelled before someone had knocked him out and threw him in the pit. The perfume had a scent unlike any scent he had ever smelled before. Cole really did not know too much about her. Studying her face like a poker player, he asked her how long ago the trading post man had killed her folks. She told him that it hurt her too much to talk about it. Cole told her it would be good to know in case they connected them to the trading post killing. Jill set the pot of stew down on the table, walked over and got Cole a plate and silverware before she sat down.

With a blank stare, she said it had been two months before, near Steamboat Springs, that her folks had been killed. Her folks fed the bastard and he just pulled out a gun, killed them and then knocked her in head. When she came to, she was tied up in the back of wagon. He got her to the trading post and she was raped by him and the two men that were with him.

Cole asked, "One more question, where did you get that perfume?"

Jill looked puzzled at Cole before she answered him, "Why are you asking me about perfume?"

"Well, I see you're upset and I figured to change the subject."

"Change it to something else!" Jill stormed, throwing her plate down on the table.

Cole eyed her for a couple of seconds. "You sure make good stew! Oh, I saw tracks of wild horses up around the creek, which reminds me, I have to haul some water over here tomorrow with that wagon in the barn." Not too much was said the rest of the night and Jill went to bed early.

Chapter 16

The next morning just after breakfast, someone knocked on the door. Cole opened the door where a man in his fifties, with a beard and big arms was standing there holding a gun. He noticed six other men standing by their horses.

Cole told him if he came to rob them, he was in for a disappointment.

The man said, "We came to get you for murder and robbery."

"Well, just who did I kill?" Cole asked.

"Mister, you talk big when there are seven of us."

Cole looked around, "Funny, I only count six. Either way you are not getting off this porch alive unless you tell me what is going on. I would not get a mile down the road before you all hanged me. Now tell me, what evidence have you got that I killed someone?"

"You had to come past the trading post to get here."

"Did that fat bastard say I robbed him? I paid good money for that black bitch. That's why he did not give me a receipt."

"So you are saying that you were at the trading post."

"Yeah, I got supplies and the man at the trading post man sold me the black woman. Then we came up here to my grandfather's place."

"We're looking for the killers of the trading post man and two others. Did you see anyone?"

"No, I have not seen anybody. I'm not surprised that someone killed the son of a bitch. Now I have answered your questions, and I am not leaving with you to be hung."

The man scratched his beard. "Mind if we look in the barn?"

"Hell no, I don't care. All you're going to see is a horse and a mule. After you all look, you'd be wise to leave."

"One more question, what your name, Mister?"

"It's Cole Turley and you're beginning to make me mad."

The man with the beard quickly put his gun away and asked, "Cole Turley, the gunfighter?"

"No. just Cole Turley, a man looking for some peace. The woman can tell you, when we left the trading post, we settled our affairs and came up here. If I had killed somebody, I sure would not come up the mountain, I would go down the mountain if I had money. It only makes sense."

"Well, Mr. Turley, we will be going; thanks for your time."

Cole stuck out his hand, "My friends call me Cole."

Cole and Jill watched them ride back down the mountain.

Jill asked Cole, "Do you think they bought it?"

Turning toward her, he said, "We'll know soon enough."

Locking the door, he walked back to table to finish his coffee.

Jill stared at him. "That man said you were a gunfighter."

Cole looked up at her. "People think what they want to think, you should know that.

Sorry for calling you a bitch, I was playing the part of someone else."

"You called me a black bitch! I know, now, what you really think of me!" she screamed.

Walking to the door, Cole replied, "I did not know it was a crime to be black."

"Well it's easy for you, to say because you're not black!" Jill spouted at him.

"You are going to let this hate destroy you. If a black man had killed your folks and raped you, would you hate black men? No, each race has good and bad people, believe me, I know! My mother was half black, half Ute Indian, and my father was Irish?"

Cole stood by the door now and told Jill to bolt it behind him because he was going out to make sure they were leaving and that he would be back later. Cole hesitated at the door and said "Do not let anybody in and that includes me, unless I give the code word of red - blue."

Cole slowly walked to the barn, looking for any movement around him and listening for any sounds. Checking on the horse and mule, he discovered his saddle that he used on Blackjack was in the tack room. He made a full circle around the cabin, always keeping the cabin in sight. He would stay close by a couple more days, to make sure they were not coming back, then he would make plans to search for Blackjack.

The sun was bright and felt good, from where he sat watching the cabin. After a couple of hours, he returned to the cabin. Knocking on the door, he waited for Jill to open the door. A few minutes later, she asked if anyone was with him, he told her no and gave the code to enter. She opened the door, stood back to let the sun shine on her naked body. Cole leaned against the door and admired her beauty.

Closing the door, he bolted it shut. Jill had boiled water in a big wooden tub. She undressed Cole without saying a word and they both climbed into the tub. She began washing Cole, and, in return, he washed her body. They kissed and made love until the water was cold.

Climbing out, they dried each other's bodies off with towels. He led her over where the bear hide was. Both of them laid down on it and continued their lovemaking. Later she rested her head on his chest and fell asleep. Cole lay there wondering if she was the one who had hit him on the head. Because if she was, she was also probably involved in killing his grandfather. He could not see a man getting the drop on him, but a woman, he could.

Cole got up and walked quietly around the room, deep in thought. By accident, he discovered a crawl hole under the big rug going below the cabin which he did not have time to check out. Someone built this in the cabin to have an exit in case someone tried to burn the cabin down or a place to hide, Cole figured. Someone must have done a lot of digging and blasting with dynamite to get it all finished. He laid back down.

Chapter 17

The next morning, Cole awakened to nd the front door open and Jill gone. He stepped out on the porch with his pistol stuck in the waist of his pants. Jill was sitting on the porch steps, drinking coffee and watching the sun rise.

"Good morning. I left the front door open to air out the cabin, I hope it did not wake you up. Do you want me to get you a cup of coffee?"

"No," Cole yawned, "I can get it."

As Cole turned to go back in, Jill whispered to Cole to turn back around. Cole turned to see the big black stallion in the clearing behind the barn. Cole watched him for a moment before he whistled for him. The black stallion reared up on his hind legs, let out a whinny, and started running toward Cole. Both man and horse were happy to be together again. Blackjack noticed Jill sitting on porch steps. He trotted over to her, stuck his cold nose to her face. Jill reached up and patted his neck. Cole said, "Blackjack is a beautiful animal and very smart."

Jill responded, "I can see why you want him."

"No," Cole said, "He's an independent free spirited horse. I let him run free, he understands me and I understand him. He's got a herd of mares up in the mountains, if he wants to go, I will not stop him."

"Cole, he is a beautiful horse. Do you think maybe I can ride him?" Jill asked.

"I'm sure he will not care after you brush him down."

When Jill returned from her ride on Blackjack, Cole was out by the barn shooting his guns. Cole could shoot with either hand, and he was practicing his quick draw. She had never seen a gunfighter getting ready for a duel before and it scared her to think Cole might get killed. Cole asked her if she would like to go to Steamboat Springs because he had some business to take care of with a man named Johnny Bell. If she wanted to stay here, he would have to haul in some water for her. In the morning, he said he was going to climb down, check out that old water well shaft that someone dug looking for water. Perhaps there was enough water there, and he wouldn't have to haul it. Actually, Cole was looking for an excuse to go down the well shaft. He figured on getting more gold out of the mine. In case something happened to him, he wanted Jill to have some money, as long as she was not involved in his grandfather's death.

Cole took a better look in the tack room inside the barn. Over in the corner, under a tarp he found a winch, some big beams, rope still in a box, and half a case of dynamite. He laid one of the big wooden beams across the well with the winch attached to it. He tied big knots in the rope every ten feet. He picked up two lanterns and four sticks of dynamite and started down into the dark pit. When the cable on the winch ran out, he tied the rope to it and slowly climbed down into the darkness. Cole sure was glad when his feet touched the ground. The first thing Cole did was light the lanterns. He walked up on the banks of the small stream to check on his grandfather grave. He had told Sill to stay locked in the house because he might use the dynamite to blast a bigger hole.

Glancing around, he found the tunnel he had dug. Crawling forward, he could smell the bear den. He dropped down quietly and saw the wall of gold. Taking a flour sack out, he began to fill it halfway full. Sticking it in the tunnel, he climbed up to push it back to where he had started. Back at the rope he picked up a lantern and walked upstream. He was surprised how big the cave was. Someone must have been digging a water well when they dug into the top of the cave. Cole found a spot where he could make a good dam and make the hole deeper and wider. That would have to wait until he got this settled with Johnny Bell. He tied the flour sack to his waist and began to pull himself out. He left one of the lanterns behind because of all the weight. Putting all the hardware back in the tack room, he hid the gold until he could put it in his saddle bag to have it checked out at Steamboat Springs.

Chapter 18

The morning Cole was heading to Steam Boat Springs, Jill decided to go along.

Blackjack showed up by the barn with a herd of mares. Cole told Jill that Blackjack was showing him what he was giving up to be with him. They came down the mountain and followed the Yampa River to Steamboat Springs. Arriving, Cole made sure Blackjack got a double order of oats and brushed down good. Cole and Jill got a room and then went to a private hot springs to relax. They both stripped down, crawled in the hot water, and made love. While at the springs, a Chinese family washed and pressed their clothes. Waiting for the clothes, they kissed and held each other tight. Returning to the hotel, they had supper in the dining room. Back in their room, Jill noticed Cole's mind was somewhere else.

Staring out the window, he asked her if she would make sure Blackjack got set free in the mountains if something happened to him. Cole strapped on his guns, and left to find Johnny Bell. Jill could have asked him not to go, but she knew if he stayed, he would not be able to live with himself.

Cole had been told by a Chinese man who had been cheated out of some money, that Johnny Bell was playing cards at the Red Bull Saloon.

Cole, with his two guns strapped on, walked in the Red Bull Saloon. The room was smoky and smelled of cheap whiskey. Cole walked up to the bar, where he could watch the poker table. Ordering a drink, he glanced around the room. He saw a woman walk out of the back room. She was a blond, built good and was very attractive. Cole was not sure who Johnny Bell was. All the Chinese man said was that he was tall with dark hair and liked to brag on himself. Trouble was there was two men playing poker who were tall and dark headed.

Cole finished his drink and was about to order another one when he smelled the perfume behind him. Turning back around, he looked into the pretty blue eyes of the blond.

"Hi, I was wondering if you would like to buy me a drink," she said, smiling at Cole.

Just at that second, one of men at the poker table yelled for her to get over by him. She hollered for him to leave her alone.

Cole said to the man, "I was going to buy my girlfriend a drink."

Johnny Bell pushed his chair back. "I'm not going to tell you twice, Mary Lou, get over here."

Cole noticed Johnny was wearing his pistols. "Hey, are those Cole Turley's pistols?"

"Yeah, I took them off him after I outdrew him and killed him."

Cole gave Johnny a cold death stare.

"Why, you must be Johnny Bell, the back shooting son of a bitch I came to kill!" The room became so quiet you could hear a pin drop.

"No one talks to me that way, Mister!" Johnny boasted. "Tell them your name so they can put it on your headstone."

"Why, Johnny Bell, don't you recognize me from the front? I'm Cole Turley coming from the grave. I'm going to kill you for the Indian woman you raped and murdered and also the old man you killed up on Han's Peak."

"Draw anytime, you son of a bitch!" Johnny just had Cole's pistols halfway out of the holster when two bullets entered his heart. Another shot followed, with a man falling from the balcony. Cole twirled around, coming face to face with his younger brother, Luke.

"Boy, you sure picked a good time to show up!" Cole stuck his hand out, to greet him.

Luke nodded his head. Cole went over to get his pistols back from Johnny Bell's body. As he was walking back toward Luke, he noticed Luke glaring at him.

"Well, I see you're still holding a grudge against me for fighting for the Union. What side I chose to fight for was my business."

Luke slammed his drink down on the table, "You know, Cole, I had a lot friends killed in that war."

"Damn it, Luke, so did I. But thank you for your help."

Luke took a big sip of whiskey, "Well big brother, I had to think about it."

"Luke, we have to talk. That old man I mentioned, that Johnny Bell killed, was Grandfather, and the woman was Ruth. We need to talk more about it, but not here. How come you happen to be here?"

"Pushing cattle up here from Texas for the miners. I got everything invested in this herd of cattle. I got a wife and little boy back home waiting on me."

About this time, things were getting back to normal in the saloon. The blond lady walked over to thank Cole for helping her out. Flirting with Cole, she asked him to come to her room for a drink.

Cole said, "You can thank me by telling me the name of your perfume and where I can get some for a girl back home."

The blond woman was shocked by Cole's answer.

"This is the first time a bottle of Midnight Mist beat me in getting a man to my room. I have to order it from New York City. My name Mary Lou. If you change your mind about that drink let me know." She was halfway across the room, when Cole tugged on her arm. "I had to act that way in front of my brother, if the offer's still good, I'll be back later."

"For you, Cole, the door is always open."

Cole and Luke walked out of the saloon to have a private conversation. Luke suggested going to Cole's room, but Cole said they couldn't go there because he had someone there. For the first time, Luke laughed, "Well, I see some things never change."

They walked into a café and ordered coffee. Luke also ordered some pie to go with his coffee. Cole told the whole story about the perfume and burying their grandfather. He had gotten all the men involved in the killing except the woman wearing that perfume. He could not kill a woman, but he was going to let her greed kill her. Cole told Luke about the wall of gold he had found.

The plan was simple; Luke would go back to the saloon the next day. He would buy drinks for everybody, and acting drunk, he would let it slip to Mary Lou that Cole had found a whole wall of gold where his grandfather was buried, but Cole would not say anymore. Cole would tell Jill the same thing and see which woman went for the gold. After that, Cole did not know what to do, but he had to know which one helped kill his grandfather.

"Cole, do I get to meet the lady in your room? She must be some lady for you to pass on the blond."

Cole answered, "That's not a bad idea. You meet her, I suggest that you and I go lave a couple drinks, because I am supposed to meet Mary Lou for a drink."

Cole got to the room, knocked on the door and said, "Hey, let me in.

Jill flung the door open. "Oh, I have been worried sick about you." Jill stood naked as a jaybird. She saw Luke behind Cole. "Dammit Cole, why didn't you tell me someone else was with you." She ran into the other room grabbing clothes to put on. A few minutes later she came back in the room fully dressed. "I am so embarrassed. Cole you should have told me someone was with you."

"He's not just someone; he's my brother. Luke this is Jill. How in hell was I supposed to know you were naked?" Cole responded.

Grinning, Luke told her, "It will be our little secret." Then he turned to Cole and said, "Hey, Cole, how about us going to have a drink or two since we have not seen each other in a long time?"

Cole's mind seemed to be somewhere else as he kept looking at Jill. "Cole, your brother's talking to you," Jill exclaimed.

"Oh, I was thinking, why don't we just have breakfast in the morning instead? Luke, you're not going back to Red Bull Saloon tonight are you?" Cole asked.

"No, I guess not. I got a room down the hall. I need to write my wife a letter, let her know I made it with the herd. I promised my son that I would." Luke answered.

"Gosh, Luke, I don't know anything about your family, what's your wife's name or your boy's name.

How long has it been since you went your way and I went mine?"

Luke pondered and said, "It's been six years, Cole. My wife's name is Peggy and my boy's name is Cole after his uncle."

Cole looked astonished, but pleased and asked how old he was.

"Four years old come May, but he acts older. I'll see you in the morning for breakfast. Try to get some sleep," Luke said as he left the room.

Cole closed the door and locked it.

Grinning at Jill, he asked her what she had on her mind. She informed him that sleeping on clean sheets was all she had on her mind. After a bit of silence, she asked Cole, "Did you find Johnny Bell tonight?"

Cole was sitting in a chair, pulling his boots off and he took his time before he answered her. "Yeah, I found him and I killed him."

Jill knew Cole did not take pleasure in killing anybody or talking about it. Jill watched Cole holding his head in his hands like he was wrestling with a problem.

"It's not over yet, is it?" she asked him.

Cole shook his head no.

"Well, let's worry about it in the morning. Right now, come to bed."

Jill threw back the covers to reveal her beautiful naked body. Cole crawled in bed with her pulling his body on top of her. She kissed him in places to arouse his body from his mind. In a few moments, the body forgot about the mind. All that mattered right now was the lust for sex as both bodies craved and demanded it. The morning and the problems could wait.

The next morning, the sun shining brightly in the room awaked Cole. Jill, already dressed, was sitting in a chair waiting for him to wake up.

"Boy, I am ready for some breakfast," he exclaimed pulling his body out of the bed. No sooner had Cole finished getting dressed, when his brother Luke knocked on the door.

They all ordered breakfast, enjoying the meal and having another cup of coffee when the blond woman walked in.

"Well, I must say, I do admire your taste in women. Is she the reason, you did not come back for that drink in my room last night?'

Jill stared at Cole as Mary Lou asked, "Can I join you for breakfast?" Before anyone could answer, she sat down and ordered coffee.

Cole was sitting between Jill and Mary Lou. He was squirming in his chair struggling to come up with a plan to leave. Before he could, Luke excused himself by saying he had matters to attend to with the buyers of his cattle. Cole was in process of standing up to depart with Luke, when each of the women, almost at the same time, pulled him back in his chair.

"Why, you can't expect two good poking women not to have a man to protect ham can you?" Mary Lou asked. "What would people say?" She was flirting with him as she rubbed his arm.

Cole said, "Well, if you will excuse me, I do have an important matter attend to. Jill, if you want, I can take you back to our room before I go."

Jill, feeling mad and jealous, said, "I can find my own way back. Besides, I want to talk to Mary Lou."

Cole got up to leave. "What's the matter, Cole, don't you think you're man enough for both of us?" Mary Lou whispered.

* * * * *

Cole went to the assessor's office to check on the value of the gold he had brought in. The little bald-headed man at the office was excited. It was the best gold he had ever seen.

He asked Cole if he wanted to file a claim.

Cole informed him, "not yet but maybe later."

Right now, he wanted to know how much the gold he had in the flour sack was worth. The little man told him, "roughly 30,000 dollars."

Even Cole was surprised at the amount. He found Luke and told him to tell Mary Lou about the gold and he was going back to the room to tell Jill about the gold.

Luke said, "Jill's not there. She moved out and got a job at the Red Bull Saloon working with Mary Lou. You do know she's in love with you. But her pride is hurt because she thinks you're not in love with her. Cole, maybe it's time to tell her how you feel."

"How I feel does not matter right now!" Cole yelled at Luke. "I have to know if she had a part in killing our grandfather. We will stick to the plan to see which one goes for the gold."

Luke said, "Okay, what are we going to do now?"

"Right now," Cole began, "we're going to the Red Bull and celebrate our good fortune."

When they got to the saloon, Cole brought the house a round of drinks.

Jill walked over to Cole to tell him that she was happy for him. She started to leave when Cole asked her where was she was going.

Jill said, "I work here, my job is to entertain the customers."

"Well, sit down, I am a customer," Cole responded.

Mary Lou came over to Cole's table with a bottle of champagne, "I hear you struck it rich. This one is on me."

"I'm not a big drinker of champagne, more of a whiskey drinker."

Mary Lou smiled, "Well, Cole, that invitation is still good. I keep my good whiskey up in my room."

Jill started to leave, when Cole grabbed her arm. "That would be rude to leave Jill out of the party, especially when she is doing such a good job of entertaining me."

"Gosh, I did not think about Jill," Mary Lou said acting a little jealous. She continued, "Why don't you take Jill out back; I have a private hot spring that I use to entertain special customers. You better take me up on it, Cole, because that fat guy with a beard at end of the bar wants Jill to entertain him and he is one of my special customers."

Cole purposely took a few minutes before he answered her. First, he thought he'd make Jill squirm a little more about what she had gotten herself into, and secondly, he did not want to show Mary Lou how much he cared about Jill. Thirdly, he knew Mary Lou was not used to being turned down. She did not like coming in second place to anyone. Cole was not used to showing his feelings, but he knew no one was taking Jill out back to the hot springs but him. It would give her time to think about the situation she had gotten herself into.

After tonight, if she wanted to work for Mary Lou, then Cole would leave her alone.

Mary Lou showed them where the hot springs was, gave them both towels, and brought them a bottle of champagne and a bottle of her finest whiskey. As soon as she went back inside, Cole and Jill took off their clothes and slipped into the hot springs. Cole grabbed her and said, "What the hell is wrong with you, working for Mary Lou? Are you crazy? She will just use you."

Jill pushed Cole away, "It's my business what I do."

Cole pulled himself out of the springs. "Well, I guess that means it's the fat man's turn to be with the bitch."

Jill said, "I didn't know it was going to be like this. Mary Lou told me just to get them to buy drinks. She told me she was out a lot of money on buying me clothes, renting a room, and buying my food. Cole, please don't go, I haven't been with anybody. Tonight is my first night. When she offered me the job, I took it because I needed money and a job, and I knew you were tired of me hanging around. I got jealous and have too much pride when you didn't want me."

"Jill, who said I didn't want you? Why in hell do you think I'm here? I will take care of Mary Lou's bill."

"Oh Cole, I will do anything to get away from here. It feels like a mountain has been lifted off my shoulders." Jill started weeping.

"Come on now, stop that, and I would be careful about saying or doing anything," Cole said, stripping off his clothes. He slipped back in, reaching for her beautiful body, they made long, hot, hard, passionate love gasping at each other's bodies.

They were still holding one another when Mary Lou came out of the darkness, naked, and jumped in the springs with them. Drunk by booze and lust she yelled, "Now we will see if you're man enough for both of us!" She grabbed Cole kissing him. Jill, not wanting to lose Cole to Mary Lou, began kissing him also. Cole was too drunk to fight off both women, or he didn't want them to stop, because he just let it happen. All three bodies became so aroused, in the heat of the moment of sexual activity caused by lust for each other's bodies, it became an orgy, each trying to outdo the other.

When the sun came up, each grabbed their own clothing and went their own ways, too embarrassed to face one another.

Chapter 18

Cole was just closing his eyes to get some much needed rest in his hotel room, when Luke started banging on his door. Cole staggered to the door, hanging on to it for support, and listened to Luke tell him Jill had gotten a ticket for the stagecoach to Denver leaving in fifteen minutes. Snapping his pants, Cole pulled out ten dollars, handing it to Luke with instructions to give it to the driver to hold the stagecoach for ten minutes while he got dressed. Cole got to the station just in time to see the driver throw off Jill's luggage and drive off down the street for Denver. Luke had his hands full trying to hold Jill back until she saw Cole coming.

"You have no right to keep me here," she yelled at Cole.

"I'm only making sure you have enough money so you will not make the same mistake again." Cole answered.

"Damn it, Cole, I just wanted to leave without having to face you again. After last night, I want to get as far away from here as I can."

"Hey, Cole, if you just give me my ten dollars, I will leave you two love birds alone, you got yourself a little wildcat. She scratched my neck!" Luke screamed.

Turning to look at his brother, Cole said, "You are charging me for helping me out?"

Grinning, Luke said, "I should, but no, I had to give the driver another ten dollars, to get her and the luggage off the stagecoach. He said that he could get fired for putting off a paying customer. Now Cole, if you just pay me, I can go and eat my breakfast."

"That's not a bad idea. Let's all go eat and figure out what we are going to do next."

Luke said, "I know what I am going to do; I'm heading for Texas and home." Luke picked up Jill's bag and all three walked to the café and Luke ordered a pot of coffee.

"Boy, this coffee is what I needed," Cole said gulping it down and pouring himself another cup.

Luke watched Cole and Jill almost drink the whole pot of coffee by themselves. Before their breakfast was served, Cole glanced up, to see Mary Lou walking in the door. "Oh no," he mumbled, causing Jill to look up into the eyes of Mary Lou as she was walking over to their table. Reaching the table, she paused, looking at Jill and then at Cole. "Well, I hope you two enjoyed our game as much I did," Mary Lou coolly said.

Luke, not knowing what she was talking about, said, "Did I miss out on something?"

"Baby, you sure did," Mary Lou continued. "I would tell you all about it, but I am late for a meeting with some friends." Looking at Cole, she told him, "You are always welcome at my place." She turned to leave and then hesitated, looked back at Jill, and said, "You sure have a pretty black ass. Wish you were not so jealous; we could have had a great time." She turned and walked over to her friends.

Jill's face flushed, and she remarked, "Something tells me that we have not seen the last of that blond bitch."

Luke glanced over at his big brother, "Well, I guess it's better if I don't know. Besides, I am heading back to Texas today unless you need me."

"No, but I'd like to talk to you about something before you leave," Cole told him.

"If you don't mind, Cole, I would like to take a nap in your room before the next stagecoach leaves," Jill said.

Cole handed the room key to Jill and said, "I was hoping to talk you into returning to the cabin with me."

"What about last night?" Jill asked.

"Hey, you think about it. If you decide not to, I will pay for your stagecoach and give you enough money to last until you find a job. Is that fair enough?" Cole asked.

"Dammit, Cole, you know I want to go with you."

"Well, take your pretty ass up to my room. I will bring your bag up when I finish talking to my brother."

"I can carry my own bag," she said smiling as she left for the room.

Cole and Luke left the cafe to check on Blackjack at the stable. "Boy, Cole, that's a beautiful black stallion. What did you want talk about?"

"Well, Luke, the other night when we were drinking, you said something about a ranch next to yours that had a big spring fed lake and the owner wanting to sell it because he was getting old."

"Yeah, the Lazy L Ranch," Luke continued. "It's got over three thousand acres, a big bunk house and a large home that's my dream home."

"Well, why don't we buy it? Besides cattle, we can run horses on it."

"Cole, I'm lucky to break even on my little ranch. I don't have that kind of money. Plus, we would need hired hands to help us."

"Luke, that gold mine is part yours. I would have never found it if I was not looking for Grandfather."

"No, Cole, that gold mine is yours, not mine."

"But Luke, I'm giving Mother's people, the Utes, a share to help guard it. I'm also giving supplies and cattle to them for the winter."

"That's fine, Cole, but I cannot accept any gold, it would not be right. It's your gold."

"Okay, Luke, if I buy the ranch, will you run it for me if I pay you?"

"What's wrong with you running it, Cole?"

"I've got to keep my eye on the gold mine."

"Cole, are you sure there is enough gold to run a big ranch and support things up here?"

"I wish you had the time to see it, Luke! I brought a half sack out, amounting to 30,000 dollars. There is a wall of solid gold, I just picked up the 30,000 dollars of gold laying on the ground. Luke, when you go home, see what the owner's bottom dollar is that he will take for the ranch. But do not tell him who the party is that is interested in the ranch. Tell him you're acting as their agent, and that's the reason they do not want to tell is that they are looking at other ranches. In the meantime, I will start taking the gold out and depositing it in the Denver bank."

"Cole, if I run your ranch, I cannot afford to keep up my ranch."

"Yes, you can, Luke, if we combine the two ranches. Keep your own brand and if your family wants, they can move into the big house. Keeping part of the cowhands at your place and maybe let the foreman live in your house."

"Sounds good, Cole," Luke continued. "The cattle are no problem, but where are we getting all the horses from?"

Reaching over, Cole patted Blackjack on the forehead and said, "Do you want to tell him, big boy, or do you want me to?"

The big black stallion whinnied and shook his head. "All right, big boy, I will tell him. Up in the mountains, Blackjack's got a big herd of mares and colts!"

"Gee, Cole, that's nice, but getting a herd of wild horses to Texas is not going to be easy. We will need men and supplies to make the trip."

Cole stated, "No, Luke, all we need is this beautiful smart stallion and me. I know horses and this horse is the smartest horse that I have ever seen. He belongs to no one but himself. Sure, I have papers on him, but he is free to roam. Jill and I will be heading out in a day or two to the cabin. I will get Lone Wolf and his people to make sure we are not followed.

A day later, Cole stopped in the general store to order supplies and buy ten repeating rifles and ammunition. When the store owner questioned his large order, Cole studied the man before he answered him. "I do not make a habit of telling someone my business, but I will this one time to ease your mind. I have men helping me with my gold mine. If you have a problem with my order, I can go somewhere else."

"No, Mr. Turley," the wife of the store owner said, "we will be glad to fill your order."

"Thank you, Madam. I just promised the men new rifles, and plenty to eat when I return from taking care of my business. You never know what this weather is going to do."

Cole tipped his hat, put on his best smile and said, "Oh, Madam, I have some unfinished business to take care of. Can you have your hired help load the wagon? I'll be back in hour."

As soon as he stepped out of store, he ran into Mary Lou. She looked almost as surprised as Cole. "Well, hello, Handsome; I was hoping to see you again without your little black she-devil."

"As a matter of fact, I was getting ready o come and see you, Mary Lou, to pay for what Jill owes you."

"Let us go to my room and discuss it?" Mary Lou suggested.

"Well, I would, Mary Lou, but Jill might kill both of us."

"Dang it, Cole, don't you find me attractive at all?"

"I think you're one of best looking women that I ever met, Mary Lou, and if we go to your room, I am afraid we could not control ourselves and Jill would kill us both."

"Come on, Cole, what she doesn't know won't hurt her." Rubbing his leg with her hand, she whispered, "I can be real bad when it comes to sex."

"Oh, Mary Lou, before you get both of us in trouble, I think you might turn around and say hello to Jill."

Mary Lou spun around and came face to face with Jill, hands on her hips, fire raging in her eyes. Smoothly,

Mary Lou said, "Why, Sweetie, we were just talking about you and the money you owe me. I offered to let him work it out for you."

Jill squinted and smiled as best as she could, "Mary Lou, one day you are going to push me too much." Turning to Cole she said, "Please, just pay her, Cole, before I lose my temper and pull out some of her dyed blond hair that she is so proud of."

"I was just trying to help you two lovebirds out. Jill, you shouldn't be so jealous of me."

Cole said, "Alright Mary Lou, if that is what you really want - I will turn Jill loose, but then you will have to fight her. Is that what you really want? If not, you better leave before my arms give out."

Mary Lou left, muttering something like, "That's the thanks I get try to help her."

The crowd of men, wanting to see a cat-fight between two women, gloomily went back into the saloon to finish their drinks.

Chapter 19

After Cole finished his business at the bank, Cole and Jill headed up the valley of the Yampa River in the wagon with Blackjack running beside them. As arranged with Lone Wolf and his warriors, they were to discourage or stop anyone from following the wagon.

When nighttime came, they would meet up with Cole to get the supplies and weapons, emptying out the wagon so, at the next town Cole came to, he could purchase more goods.

This happened every time Cole came across enough goods to fill the wagon. Cole would signal Lone Wolf with a mirror by day or fire at night. By the time, they reached the cabin, the Indians would have supplies for the winter and at least thirty repeating rifles. Cole's plan was to set up a dummy mine along the upper valley of the Yampa River, making people think that was where the gold mine was. They would leave the wagon behind with the Indians guarding the dummy mine.

Cole and Jill, with the pack mules, pushed on to the cabin. Arriving four days later in the evening, Jill fixed supper, while Cole attended to the mules and Blackjack.

In Steamboat, Cole had met an old man who was an engineer. He drew up some plans for Cole on how to get the water up to the surface, so Cole would not have to haul water from the creek. Cole left the equipment for the well in the barn. He would start on it in the morning.

Right now, he wanted to get some hot food and a good night's sleep. It still bothered him about the smell of that perfume. And things have a way of showing the truth sooner or later. In his heart, he could not see Jill being a party to murder. Until he knew better, he would believe what she told him.

* * ** *

During the couple months they were on the mountain, Cole had built a device that pumped water up into a large rock tub beside the well. It was kind of like a windmill, but he had to hand pump the water into the big rock tub that he had built using the rocks nearby and mortar to seal the rock tub. Cole had made a small platform using pulleys to get him up and down into the cave making it easy to bring out the gold. With the opening of the water shaft bigger than normal, Cole had no problem with room.

Cole had brought out somewhere between $200,000 to $300,000 in gold and buried it close to the barn under a manure pile.

Lone Wolf and his braves were supposed to be up the mountain sometime in the middle of the month, to help guard the gold on their way to the bank.

Cole had not seen too much of Blackjack, for he was roaming the mountain with a herd of wild horses. So

Cole was surprised one morning when he was eating breakfast and Jill ran inside to tell him Blackjack was outside. She had been getting a bucket of water for drinking when he ran up.

Cole could tell something was not right, when Blackjack kept stomping the ground with his hooves and letting out a whinny sound. Cole asked him if someone was coming, when his big head went up and down Cole knew the big stallion was warning him. Jill looked on in amazement as Cole asked him how many riders. The big stallion took his hoof and hit the ground ten times. Cole hugged the big stallion and told him to go before they arrived. Grabbing Jill, he pushed her in the house along with the bucket of water and bolted the door. He pulled a chair over by the window, staring out into the still morning.

Jill watched him for a while before she asked Cole if that horse really could warn them. He told her that she better bet he can, and he hoped it was just Lone Wolf and his people. He thought they were coming a little earlier than they were supposed to come. A couple of hours passed without any sign of company. Jill started to grow impatient sitting on the floor. As she started to stand up, a bullet tore into the room. Hitting the floor, she looked scared, and, crawling over to Cole, she asked him who he thought it might be. It was not long before she got her answer.

"Hey Cole, how's that black bitch been treating you?" Both Jill and Cole looked at each other. They recognized Mary Lou's voice.

"What do you want, Mary Lou?" Cole shouted out.

"I want all your gold and you, Cole," she replied.

"Well come and get it, Mary Lou, but I think you all are in for a big disappointment, there is no gold here!" Cole yelled.

"I know, Cole, we figured out where the gold is. Down the well shaft where they threw you."

"What do you mean 'they? I smelled your perfume when you hit me from behind. You helped kill my grandfather."

"No, Cole, you got it all wrong. Ask your black bitch. She knows."

Cole turned to face Jill with hate in his eyes, asking her. "what do you know about this?"

Jill's eyes were wide with terror, for it was the first time she had ever witnessed the hate Cole held in his body. "I swear that she is lying, Cole. I know nothing of your grandfather's murder and I sure in hell did not hit you."

Cole barked, "What is she supposed to know, Mary Lou?"

"She knows the two men you killed at the trading post. One was a cross-dresser who liked to dress as a woman and he stole my perfume." Jill was boiling mad, yelling.

"What the hell's that got to do with murder?"

"That cowboy bragged to me that he helped throw this gunslinger down a shaft leaving him to die."

Mary Lou continued, "Hey Cole, how did you get out of there? It would be nice to know before we blow you and your black sweetie to hell. Don't you think you owe me that much since I solved the perfume mystery for you?"

"Well, Mary Lou, I doubt if you would believe me if I told you."

"Oh, Cole, we got the cabin surrounded, so tell me; it's not like you all are going anywhere."

Cole motioned for Jill to pull the big rug back while he kept their attention talking. Jill saw the trapdoor under the cabin and grabbed some food, water, and a rifle with ammunition.

She cussed Cole calling him a son of a bitch for not trusting her. Cole noticed a guy sneaking up to the cabin, so he raised his rifle and fired, and watched as his body rolled to a stop. Cole did not have to tell Jill to crawl into the hole, because all their rifles started firing at the cabin. Cole saw another person advancing on the cabin, so he dropped him with a bullet to his chest. When the rifle fire slowed down, he yelled at Mary Lou, "What's the matter, Mary Lou, don't you want to know, how I got out of that water grave?" He waited a minute for her to answer him, but heard nothing. Finally, Cole said, "I was raised by Ute Indians who taught me how to change into an eagle and fly. I flew right out of that water grave."

His story did not impress anyone as they charged the cabin. Two of the men had sticks of dynamite. Cole dropped one with a shot to the head, but the other man managed to throw his dynamite on the roof. Cole scrambled for the trap door before the dynamite exploded.

Cole just got the door closed when the roof came tumbling down and the cabin caught on fire. Whoever built the cabin must have dug the small basement. It was a room about the size of eight-by-eight feet with a shelf on one wall. On the shelf were four candles and couple of rusty cans. On the opposite wall was a tunnel. Cole did not know where it went.

Whoever built the cabin, must have liked to dig. There was the basement with the tunnel and the big shaft they threw him down. Whoever it was, one thing for sure, had to be an expert with explosives to get all this accomplished.

Cole whispered to Jill to stay put, while he checked out the tunnel. He took a candle for light to see, and with his rifle, he crawled forward. Cole crawled about two hundred feet When he heard voices up ahead. Putting out his candle, he slowly moved forward to where the voices were coming from. He crawled another two hundred feet before he saw light ahead.

Reaching the end of the tunnel, he looked down into the cave. The voices were Mary Lou and three men who had come down the shaft looking for the gold. One of the men found the entrance to where the gold was located. Cole lay watching from his perch in the cave, when one of men returned with a chunk of gold from the tunnel. Excited, he told the others about a whole wall of gold he had seen.

Without a warning, Mary Lou and one of the men pulled out pistols and shot the other two men. Still hanging onto the chunk of gold, the man looked very surprised as he fell over dead. The men up above yelled down, asking what was the shooting about. The remaining man yelled up to the men telling them they had shot some snakes. They were going to check out a tunnel in the cave and to make sure they guarded the opening. One of the men asked what was there to guard because no one was there. No sooner had he said it, he was stuck in the chest with an arrow, the other three men fell dead soon after him. Lone Wolf and his braves had been hunting for elk when they heard the explosion.

In the meantime, Mary Lou and her accomplice crawled to the gold in search of a fortune. They both dropped into the other cave to look at the wall of gold. Mary Lou ran her hands across the wall of gold, at same time planning to do her partner in. She would wait until the couple got closer to Steamboat to make that move. She still needed him to help get rid of the other four men. The man let out a loud yell of joy for finding the gold. That was a big mistake, waking the big grizzly bear that was asleep in the back of the cave.

They did not know the bear was in the cave until he came at them. Both scrambled for the tunnel opening and they might have made it, but they panicked. Pushing each other away from the opening, both were doomed to die by the big grizzly. It was a painful death as the grizzly bear ripped them to shreds scattering body parts and blood around the cave. By the lime Cole heard the screams and got to them, it was too late to save them. He backed out of tunnel into the hands of Lone Wolf who had come down to help when he heard the screams. The Ute Indians worshiped bears, and when Lone Wolf told his braves about the big grizzly bear killing the ones who were evil, the braves began praising the bear.

In the meantime, Cole rushed over to what was left of the cabin to rescue Jill. He hollered for Lone Wolf to help him lift the big burned beam off the trapdoor allowing him to raise the trapdoor. Down in the corner of the room was Jill, scared but alright. When she got to the top of the stairs, Cole grabbed her and carried her out of the burning cabin. Cole told Jill the fate of Mary Lou and about the bear. Her greed had gotten the best of her; she had been killed for the love of gold. Her accomplices were buried out back of the burned cabin by the deep ravine. That is, everyone except Mary Lou and the man in the cave for there was not much to bury with the waking of the big grizzly bear. When the bear left the cave in the spring, Cole would get what remains were left and bury them. Cole noticed Jill standing outside the burned cabin. Talking to no one, just thinking out loud, she remarked it sure was a nice cabin.

Cole gazed at her beautiful body. "It sure was," he remarked. "I have a lot of good memories. Oh Jill, did I ever tell you about my son who is 16-years-old and living with my sister in Indian Territory?"

Jill turned sharply around and glared into Cole's brown eyes. "No, you must have forgotten to tell me, Cole, about having a son who is sixteen!" she answered with a sharp edginess in her voice.

"Well, dammit, Jill, you're not making this easy."

"Oh, hell, Cole, I'll make it easy for you to get rid of me. I will leave just as soon we get to a town."

"Boy, I'll never understand women," Cole screamed. "I am trying to ask you to be my wife, for God's sakes. I thought you should know about my son before I asked you to marry me. Gosh, I have plans on rebuilding the cabin three times bigger than what it was, but if we don't get married, I guess I'll just get drunk."

"Cole, you're asking me to marry you?" Jill yelled happily at him.

"Well, yeah, that was the idea if you will have me."

"Darn, Cole, you sure are not the romantic type, but the answer is yes, I'll be your wife."

"Okay. After we get the gold to Denver and send Luke some money to buy a ranch, we will get married, if that is alright with you, Jill. But I have to go to Indian Territory and tell Mary about Grandfather."

"We'll both go, Cole. I'd like to meet your family," Jill told Cole.

Lone Wolf, who had been within earshot, spoke, "It seems like she is already giving you orders, Cole, just like a woman does so you better get used to it." A hint of a smile shown on Lone Wolf's wise face.

"Have you got your list of supplies that you and the tribe need?" Cole asked Lone Wolf. "Can I hire some of your people to camp here and watch things until we get back from Indian Territory?"

Lone Wolf answered, "Do not worry, my blood brother, we will camp here and I will send some braves to watch the other mine. Some of the young braves would like rifles like the older braves have."

"Tell them they will get rifles but they must not make war with the white man," Cole told Lone Wolf. "They must use them only to defend themselves."

Chapter 20

As the years went by, Cole kept his promise to Jill. He built a big house where the cabin once was, but first he made the basement a lot bigger so he could store the gold. Rumor was there was millions in gold taken from the bear's den. But with the Ute Indians guarding the mountain, no one dared to go up the mountain, and, if you did, you better be invited.

Cole sent gold to his sister in Indian Territory to build a bigger ranch. Mary lived with them until she died of old age. Cole's son, Sam, came to Colorado to help Cole and Blackjack drive a bunch of wild horses to Texas where Cole and Luke's ranch was. Cole picked out a young stallion who looked like Blackjack, and gave him to Sam. He stayed to help break the wild horses at their big ranch in Texas. Sam had a way with horses, like his father did.

Cole returned to Colorado, buying up a lot of land around where the cabin stood, making sure Lone Wolf and his people had a place to live in peace. Cole and Jill would have ten children, six boys and four girls who gave them thirty-two grandchildren in their lifetime.

The old gunfighter finally found peace with himself. The gunfighter and the big black stallion would become a legend. It is said a big black stallion still roams the mountains of Colorado in search of his master.

After fighting in the Civil War, Cole Turley was forced to become a gunfighter to avenge the killing of his loved ones while he was away.

Together with his big black stallion, Blackjack, the two of them become a legend of the Old West.

www.ingramcontent.com/pod-product-compliance
Lightning Source LLC
Chambersburg PA
CBHW051430150726
48000CB00005B/2038